W9-AGN-306

Taking Off

TAKING OFF. Copyright ©1995 by Merlyn's Pen, Inc. All rights reserved. Except as permitted under the United States Copyright Act, no part of this publication may be reproduced or distributed in any form or by any means, or stored in a data base or retrieval system, without the prior written permission of the publisher except in the case of brief quotations embedded in critical articles and reviews.

Published by Merlyn's Pen, Inc.
4 King Street
P.O. Box 1058
East Greenwich, Rhode Island 02818-0964

Printed in the United States of America

These are works of fiction. All characters and events portrayed in this book are fictional, and any resemblance to real people or incidents is purely coincidental.

Cover design by Alan Greco Design
Cover illustration by Tim Greene. Copyright ©1996

Library of Congress Cataloging-in-Publication Data
Taking off : and other coming of age stories by American teen writers
    / edited by Kathryn Kulpa.
        p.   cm. -- (The American teen writer series)
    "All of the short stories in this book originally appeared in
    Merlyn's pen"--Acknowledgments.
        Summary: Here are thirteen short stories by teens and for teens
    about the coming-of-age experience.
        ISBN 1-886427-02-X : $9.75
        1. Short stories, American.   2. Children's writings, American.
    3. Youths' writings, American.   [1. Short stories.   2. Children's
    writings.   3. Youths' writings.]   I. Kulpa, Kathryn.   II. Series.
    PZ5. T18   1995
    [Fic]--dc20   94-48919
                                                                   CIP
                                                                   AC

99 98 97 96   6 5 4 3 2

Taking Off

AND OTHER COMING OF AGE STORIES BY AMERICAN TEEN WRITERS

Edited by
Kathryn Kulpa

The American Teen Writer Series
Editor: R. James Stahl

Merlyn's Pen, Inc.
East Greenwich, Rhode Island

Acknowledgments

All of the short stories in this book originally appeared in *Merlyn's Pen: The National Magazines of Student Writing.*

The following stories are copyright © by Merlyn's Pen, Inc.: "Taking Off" by Kristen Binck, "A Start" by Elizabeth Buhot, "Frostee" by Roper Cleland, "Dandelion Chains" by Sarah Manvel, and "Sisters, Friends, and Enemies" by Curtis Sittenfeld.

The following stories are copyright © by the individual authors: "The Nauga Hunters" by Matthew Cheney, "Nightgowns" by Asma Hasan, "Fish Summer" by Michael Lim, "Sing Softly, Wind" by Diane Matous, "Curse of the Sea Lord" by Tricia Owens, "The View from Downstairs" by John Peters, "The Ultimatum" by Kris Reich, "Summer's End" by Jeanine Skendzel, and "Memoirs of a 13-Year-Old" by Willie Turnage.

The American Teen Writer Series

Young adult literature. What does it mean to you?

Classic titles like *Lord of the Flies* or *Of Mice and Men*— books written by adults, for adult readers, that also are studied extensively in high schools?

Books written for teenagers by adult writers admired by teens—like Gary Paulsen, Norma Klein, Paul Zindel?

Or shelves and shelves of popular paperbacks about perfect, untroubled, blemish-free kids?

Titles like *I Was a Teenage Vampire? Lunch Hour of the Living Dead?*

The term "young adult literature" is used to describe a range of exciting literature, but it has never accounted for the stories, poetry, and nonfiction actually written by young adults. African American literature is written by African Americans. Native American stories are penned by Native Americans. The Women's Literature aisle is stocked with books by women. Where are the young adult writers in young adult literature?

Teen authors tell their own stories in *Merlyn's Pen: The National Magazines of Student Writing.* Back in 1985 the magazine began giving young writers a place for their most compelling work. Seeds were planted. Ten years later, The American Teen Writer Series brings all of us the bountiful, rich fruit of their labors.

Older readers might be tempted to speak of these authors as potential writers, the great talents of tomorrow. We say: Don't. Their talent is alive and present. Their work is here and now.

Contents

About the Author Profiles:

The editors of The American Teen Writer Series have decided to reprint the author profiles as they appeared in *Merlyn's Pen* when the authors' works were first published. Our purpose is to reflect the writers' ages, grade levels, and interests at the time they wrote these stories.

The Nauga Hunters

by MATTHEW CHENEY

Hank, a thirteen-year-old boy with wispy brown hair and spindly legs, spotted his little brother sitting on the floor of the living room, watching a cartoon.

"Hey, Chucky, wanna go nauga hunting?" asked Hank.

"What's a nauga?" asked Chucky, turning away from the television.

"A nauga's a little thing—'bout the size of a cat—that has big long teeth and a red feather for a tail," explained Hank, with the appropriate hand movements.

"A featha for a tail?"

"Yup. And naugas can change color so we can't see 'em, 'cept for the tail; that don't change color."

"How we gonna hunt the naugas then, if we don't see nothin' but the tail?"

"Well, we'll hafta look all over the woods, and if we see a red tail movin', then we'll shoot it."

"I don't wanna shoot it."

"Aw, come on, Chucky, ya gotta shoot naugas."

"Why can't we jus' keep 'im for a pet?"

" 'Cause naugas eat people."

"Oh. What if he got to like me?"

"Naugas don't like nobody."

"Nobody?"

"Nobody. So, you gonna come nauga hunting with me or not?"

"You sure they don't like nobody? I mean, the Tylers' dog likes me, and he don't like nobody."

"Naugas don't like nobody. Period. Now, I'll give you five seconds to make up your mind. One. Two. Three—"

"Nobody?"

"Come on, Chucky! I told you they don't like nobody. Now, you comin' or not?"

"I'll come."

"Good. Now, let's go up to my room and get the water guns."

Hank filled his black Colt water gun in the bathtub while Chucky filled his bright green Luger in the sink. They pressed the white plastic plugs into the filling holes and stuck the guns into the holsters that were attached to their belts.

Hank put his camouflage army cap onto his head. "I wanna cap!" came Chucky's high-pitched scream.

"I don't have another."

"Then I'll go get Dad's."

"It won't fit."

"My butt it won't."

"OK. Don't say I didn't tell ya, 'cause I did tell ya."

Chucky waddled down the stairs and Hank followed shortly. He was carrying an old backpack that had been sitting in his closet since the beginning of time.

Chucky was downstairs in the den closet. Hank couldn't see his little brother in the shadows of the closet, but every now and then a coat or a hat or a boot would fly out and land on the floor amidst a pile of other coats, hats, and boots.

"Chucky! Whatcha cleanin' out the closet for?!"

"Gotta find a hat."

"Dad's is right here. What's wrong with Dad's? Thought that was the one you wanted."

"Don't fit."

"I told ja so. Come on, the naugas'll be hibernatin' soon."

Chucky climbed over a pile of coats that lay before him and stood looking at Hank. "Ain't got a hat."

"Chucky, will you come on! I try to be nice to you for once and whatta you do? You just say, 'I ain't got a hat,' like I really care. Here, take mine." Hank angrily took off his cap and hit Chucky in the chest with it. Chucky took it. "Now pick up these clothes and let's get goin' already!"

The sky was clear of clouds and birds. It was a blue that can only be seen on brisk autumn days, a Pacific blue. The air was vivacious, the trees lit with the color of their leaves, the hills a massive fruit salad.

"I don't see no naugas," said Chucky.

"You won't for a little while. We ain't deep 'nough inta the woods yet."

Chucky crackled along behind his brother.

"Will you stop stepping on all the leaves! You'll scare the naugas away."

"Didn't mean to."

"I don't care if you meant to or not, just be quiet. Some hunter you are."

They plodded together through the woods like a pair of senile tigers. Then Hank stopped and held up his left hand. He pulled his Colt out of its holster. "Nauga," he whispered.

"Where?"

He pointed to a wet, rotting log that lay across a small trench.

"In there?" asked Chucky.

"Yup. Now, he don't know we've seen him, so be wicked quiet and walk up there, onto the hill, just so you're looking over the hole. I'm gonna try ta flush 'im out."

"You sure I gotta go there alone?"

"Wimp."

"OK, I'll go. *Sheesh*."

Hank snuck forward, very quietly, and peeked under the log. He heard his little brother walking above him. "There it goes!" screamed Hank. "Shoot it!" He looked up as Chucky squirted water in all directions. Then he brought up his plastic Colt and squirted Chucky.

"Hey!" exclaimed Chucky, the thin blasts of water still hitting him. Hank lowered his gun. "Whatcha do that for?"

"You're stupid. You really believed in naugas? Prob'ly believe in dragons and Santa Claus, too."

"Huh? What's wrong 'bout Santa?"

"Ain't no such thing! No Santa and no naugas, stupid!"

"Then why'd ja take me out here then?"

"I dunno."

"C'mon, Hank. Why? We got all dressed up an' stuff an' then there ain't no naugas? Why?"

"It ain't important."

"You jus' wanted ta trick me, that's all. Jus' wanted me ta look stupid."

"No. No, that weren't it."

"Come on then, tell me." He waited for a moment, but Hank made no move to answer. "I'll tell Mom. I'll tell her you tricked me and took me out here jus' ta get me wet. I'll tell her you threw me in the brook. I'll tell her you jus' wanted me ta get peenamonia." Hank walked away from Chucky and sat on a damp rock.

"I'm goin' home," said Chucky.

"Then go on."

"Hank, why'd ja take me out here? C'mon, I won't tell nobody."

Silence. Chucky again: "Is it about Sally?"

"No, 'course not."

"I betcha broke up with her and you jus' wanted ta take it out on me."

"I woulda beaten you up then."

"Is it about school? You mad 'cause you got a bad grade or somethin'?"

"No. I'm use ta bad grades. Listen, jus' go home. I'll be back in a while."

Chucky stood next to his brother without saying anything. Then he asked quietly, "Is it about Mom and Dad?"

"Jus' beat it!"

"What's gonna happen? Is Dad gonna leave?"

"You wanna know? You really wanna know, you little jerk? Las' night I heard Mom and Dad talkin'."

"Fightin'?"

"Nope, jus' talkin'. Dad said he's gonna leave and go ta New York and take me, and Mom can have you. So I brought you out here jus' ta be nice 'cause I may never really be able ta do anythin' like this again. OK? Satisfied?"

"You sure yer tellin' the truth?"

Hank stood up and jumped on his brother; they fell to the damp ground. His eyes were sparkling and his lips were unfirm. "Would I lie about that, you little . . ." His voice faded as he pulled his arm up to punch Chucky. Chucky was crying now. Hank stood up. "Forget it," he said. "Supper'll be almost ready." Chucky was still on the ground. "You comin'?"

Chucky pulled himself up and brushed off his rear end. His face was streaked with tears. "Yup," he said softly.

"Well, hurry up. Then after supper maybe we can go hunt some more naugas. They ain't invisible at night."

"Thought you said they ain't real—like dragons."

"You believed me? Boy, maybe you *are* stupider than you look." He turned around and headed for home, his little brother trying to keep up.

About the Author

Matthew Cheney lives in Plymouth, New Hampshire, and reports, "I've collected about 40 rejection letters over the past two years, but by the time 'Nauga Hunters' is published I'll probably have 50." Besides writing, he enjoys soccer, science fiction, and "watching Citizen Kane *over and over and over." He wrote this story while in the eighth grade at Newfound Memorial Middle School in Bristol, New Hampshire.*

Nightgowns

by ASMA HASAN

MILLIE'S STORY

It was deathly hot at Austin, and the beginning of the school year. All the Fourth Formers, sophomores in normal language, came back early to go on this retreat; we were supposed to become acquainted with the others. The campus was quiet and empty, nothing like its usual state. Prize Day of last June was still in my mind: Candice Bergen's commencement speech (the closest I had ever come to a celebrity), packing everything up, the dictionaries that were supposed to be prizes, the long, long handshaking line. I couldn't believe we were back already. I ran around with the old girls, laughing, saying, "Let's check our mailboxes." I felt sorry for the new girls; they all stood around with shifty looks on their faces, arms crossed at their waists. I wondered which of the new girls was my roommate. Some of the new girls were wearing flashy, fancy jewelry and had permed hair. I smiled to myself, knowing that Austin would change them and by Parents' Weekend they would all have straight hair and simple silver earrings.

For the most part, I hadn't changed to the Austin norm. I had dark brown hair, which I kept very short and never lightened. I wore what I liked, much beyond J. Crew, and hated Birkenstocks. I wore glasses because contacts were too much of a pain, and I would have to wake up fifteen minutes earlier to put them in my eyes. That never bothered the other girls there, who could stay up all night and function normally the next day. Maybe all this was why I had had trouble finding a roommate.

The retreat was average. We went swimming a lot. All the girls wore turquoise one-piece swimsuits. The daring ones wore orange or fuchsia suits; their muscular legs stuck out like pencils with knobs in the middle. Kyra was the only one in a bikini; she was obviously a new girl—no one wore a bikini in front of the guys. I thought she was nice, cutesy with her dark eyes and blondish hair. She was skinny and had a little perky nose. I had no idea that she was my roommate.

I was surprised at her excitement at being my roommate; she had been so quiet at the retreat. Later somebody who was in her cabin during the retreat told me that she had thought Kyra was a social climber; I didn't think so. We set up the room, her bed by the window, mine in the corner, tapestries and black and white posters on the walls. Pre-season sports began, and we didn't see much of each other, running around to practices and meals.

Suddenly it became cold and classes had already begun. All my classes were surprisingly hard, and I went to bed late on school nights for the first time in two and a half years. Kyra and I liked each other, and we became good roommates; she didn't party in our room, and I didn't talk about her behind her back.

We had that unspoken understanding. We would lie in bed at night and tell each other our secrets— who we thought was hot; which girls were pretty or snobby; who was smart. We would talk about our flirtations; Kyra did most of the talking. She was the first roommate I had ever had.

We started playing this game in which one of us would describe the other out loud. Kyra would always say that my nose was soft and round (she was too nice to say that it was big), and that my lips were thick and round. I would always avoid describing Kyra; I was afraid that too much of my admiration of her would seep out.

Kyra had made a lot of friends, even with the old people. I remember in the beginning thinking that it was nice she had made so many friends, even with seniors. I was sort of condescending. Then I realized she was more popular than I was; she had made greater progress in three months than I had in two and a half years! She was even better friends with some of the girls I had known since Second Form, eighth grade in normal language. I wasn't upset, just surprised. People were coming to visit Kyra, addressing the notes on the door to her.

Kyra's grades weren't as good as mine, at least I don't think they were. I would just see a few grades on wisps of paper here and there. It was a comfort to me, though, to be able to think that I was at least smarter than she in school, that those two years had paid off for something. But I secretly thought to myself that my grades could not be *that* much better.

One night after Kyra spent a short half-hour describing me, I had to describe Kyra; I had been avoiding it for too long. I started out with the normal sort of thing:

"Your hair is really nice. It's a nice type of shiny and soft. You have pretty eyes; they're like brown glass. Your nose is perfect, like a little button but with a small peak in the middle. Your ears are a little small, but not too small. Your face is round, well—more oval-shaped, like a mask."

Then I started to really let go.

"Well, everything about you is really perfect. I mean, I even admire your feet. Your toes aren't stubby like mine. Your fingers are long and skinny, like your legs. And your knees are perfect too; they're not flat and wrinkly like mine. Yours are smooth and heart-shaped."

I waited for some sort of response. I paused to give her the chance to answer, to accept what I divulged, so I would not go any further. But she never answered.

"What I'm really trying to say, Kyra, is that I really . . . admire you. I mean . . . I guess I want to *be* you. I really want to be you. Everyone likes you; the guys think you're hot, and the girls always tell you their secrets and say that they want to have a body like yours. See . . . I guess I feel that after two and a half years, I should be above your level, but I'm really below it. You have to understand; I don't obsess over you or anything. I would just like to be like you. Is that weird?"

I let out a gasp of air; it had taken a lot of guts, or stupidity, to explain myself like that. I was scared of her reaction, but I wanted to hear it. "Kyra, are you

there? Are you listening?" I realized suddenly that Kyra
was asleep, that she hadn't heard anything I had said,
that she was sleeping quietly, lying there in the dark,
in her nightgown.

KYRA'S STORY

I was really nervous about Austin. In addition to
being racked with nerves, I also had to leave home
three days earlier than usual to go on this retreat. The
purpose of the retreat was for all of us to become
friends—teacher-type reasons. I stood watching all the
old students run around and hug each other, saying
things like, "Can you tell I've lost weight?" "Do you
like my haircut?"

I pretended to be very interested in scratching my
elbows and yawning—too cool for all this. I don't even
think anyone noticed. I took a sort of quantitative look
at the old girls. They all wore J. Crew, preppie clothes.
I was relieved; I wore the same type of clothes. The
girls were pretty skinny. Most of them were blond.
They all looked the same, though. Millie looked different from everyone. She had black hair, glasses, and
wore red shorts. Nobody wore red shorts. It was just
one of those things. She looked good in them.

I'm glad the retreat was organized. There were times
when I was so homesick; I never could have managed
being in classes right away. I remember a time, during
one of our few hours of free time—the nightly bonfire—that I just felt like crying. It just so happened
that Millie was sitting there. She told me corny jokes
and laughed at them herself; it cheered me up, in a
strange way. The next day we went swimming. I was

the only one wearing a bikini; I whispered to Millie, remembering the red shorts, about how weird I felt. She said that I should feel happy that I was the only one skinny enough to wear a bikini. I noticed Sara, a really pretty girl in my cabin, and hung out with her. The guys were all over her! All the girls were pretty, in their own way. Millie wasn't really pretty, though; she was different looking. I had no idea that she was my roommate.

I was so happy when I found out she was my room-mate; I was glad I hadn't been stuck with some geek. Sara was in my dorm, too. I liked the dorm for the most part. I insisted on having my bed by the window; afterwards, I felt a little guilty, but Millie didn't com-plain. I later learned that Millie really wasn't a com-plainer; she would never raise her voice for anything. I didn't see much of her during pre-season sports; I was running around trying to organize myself.

It got cold, and I had to use my wool sweaters sooner than I thought. My classes required a lot of work, but I was in bed at precisely 10:30 on week-nights. Millie would stay up all night, it seemed, but she would oversleep the next day. Sometimes she would study in the bathroom so as not to bother me. She was caring and did nice things like that. When I wanted to party, I would go to Sara's room or someone else's room; I respected Millie for not drinking. There were so many things Millie was outgoing about, and there were other things that she wasn't outgoing about at all. She didn't talk to the guys at all; she didn't avoid them or anything, but she didn't especially make an effort.

Once when I was sitting at a lunch table, I was doing the normal girl flirt thing, laughing at what the guys said. Then Will, this tall blond kid, said something about my "gurn roommate." I wasn't sure what it meant, but I said, "She just studies a lot." Will said, "Admit it; she's a geek." He had a smug smile on his face like he was winning points with Sara and me. I stood up and slammed the bowl I was holding down on my tray. I nervously yelled at him:

"Look, Millie is a great roommate. She is nice, considerate and caring. She would never say what you just said about anybody, whether she liked them or not. And at least she has the confidence and individuality to avoid wearing stuff like that ugly J. Crew Rugby you're wearing."

I was glad I did that. It made me feel good—even if the guys called me a bitch for a week.

That was the night I started playing this game with Millie. I never told her about Will, but I wanted to build up her confidence. One of us would describe the other out loud, saying her nice features. I would tell her she was skinny and had good muscle tone. I wondered if I sounded fake. She would always say she was sleepy and would never describe me.

Once I started drinking, I was accepted into this circle of people, popular people. Practically every Saturday night, Sara and I, other girls too, would sneak over to the guys' dorm next door. We wouldn't be running up and down the hall with beer or anything, but we would go to a guy's room and play chandeliers. The next day, the guy whose room I had been in would come up to me and put his hands on my shoulders and make some funny comment. It was great. I had made all these friends through drinking. I never lost control like Sara did, though; I think she would actually have sex with some guys. I would always leave when someone passed out because things were too serious then. I didn't want to be involved.

All the girls took a liking to me right away. They borrowed clothes from me, never from Millie. She told me she liked it that way. I wonder if she noticed that the girls were making efforts to talk to me and not her. I didn't want her to be envious. She didn't show any emotions, though. She was really smart, everyone told me; I knew she worked hard for her grades.

One night, Millie finally said she would describe me. She starts going on about my hair and eyes, normal stuff. I am feeling sleepy. Then she says something about a mask, and I open my eyes. Then I hear that I am perfect, and so are my toes and knees. How strange! Millie was kind of comparing herself to me.

Then the talking ceases. I close my eyes. I figure Millie is done. Then she starts into this long speech about how she wants to be me, or admires me or something. I open my eyes. It sounds kind of like she's obsessing over me, but then she says she's not. I'm scared for some reason; I don't even want to breathe. How am I supposed to react to that? Why would she want to be me? People are always telling me if they think I have gained weight, or if they have a better grade on a test than me—not stuff like Millie was telling me.

There's just quiet then. Millie asks if I can hear her, if I'm there. I close my eyes. I don't answer because I don't want Millie to know that I know she looks up to me so much. It's embarrassing. So I just lie there, not saying anything. I know she wants me to say something, but I act like I'm asleep and nervously pick at the seam in my nightgown.

ABOUT THE AUTHOR

Asma Hasan comes from Pueblo, Colorado, and attends Groton School in Groton, Massachusetts. She wrote this story while in the tenth grade. She admits to "an incredible rush" from public speaking, and recently won the Richard K. Irons Public Speaking Prize. Future joys will include "traveling the world—especially Thailand, because that's where W. Somerset Maugham lived, and Italy because I love pasta."

Summer's End

by JEANINE SKENDZEL

Our rusting station wagon faithfully rolls past the monotonous wheat fields. The billboards are now less densely grouped from mile to mile, forcing me to stop counting them out of pure boredom. Fifty-seven signs ago we were home in Landview. Now we're heading to our cottage on Scenic Lake. A dull ache pounds in my head and my stomach churns in rhythm with the motor. I stretch out comfortably halfway across the seat until I accidentally hit my sleeping sister, Tracy. Just a few months ago we could hardly fit in this back seat: that's when my brother, Drew, was here. He would take up half the seat alone. The pain stabs me and the memories quickly flood back.

We're diving for Drew's waterproof wristwatch as we do every year. One of us throws the watch as far as possible and the other person dives to find it. Since Drew is seventeen and I'm only fourteen, he holds an unfair advantage, but I never complain. This time it's my turn to throw it. He has already beaten me three times today by thirty seconds each, so this particular time I secretly throw the watch behind me. Drew bobs up and down the dock, searching for a glint of silver in the hot summer sun.

"Come on, Ben! What'd ya do with it?" he frustratedly whines. I foolishly grin back, pleased that I have finally outwitted him at something. Grabbing my arm, he strongly twists it into a horrible snakebite.

"Tell me, Ben, or you know what's coming," he whispers, checking for our parents. We glare at each other, flashing our ugliest poses. Finally, we break down laughing and I point happily toward the watch.

"You little . . ." is all I hear before he sprints off the dock and pulls into a flawless dive.

Usually he's able to grab it right away, but this time he remains underwater for a long time. I move down the dock to where I'm standing directly above him. He isn't squirming and his hand isn't groping. I figure he's getting me back for tricking him, showing off how much better he is than me. But then I notice his head curved in an awkward position, and I realize he isn't joking. Frantically I jump into the cool, neck-deep water, momentarily stunned and unable to help my own brother.

"Mom! Dad! Come quick! Something's wrong with Drew!"

Both my parents run wildly over. Dad pushes heavily through the water and Mom's feet pound on the rickety dock. Mom falls to her knees, weak and faint as she spots her son crumpled on the bottom.

"Ben!" Dad shouts. "Hold his mouth above water while I call . . ." Then he's gone, bounding up to our cottage, three steps at a time.

Drew's skin is cold and leathery, even though it's eighty degrees out. I feel sick and I notice my hands trembling, shaking Drew's fragile head. I can't believe this is happening. I can't believe it . . . I can't believe it . . .

"Move it, Ben! You're squishing me," Tracy shrieks, pounding my shoulder with her fists and pulling me back to the present. Tracy's only seven years old and doesn't understand anything yet.

"Sorry, Trace," I mumble, and slide back against the vinyl door. Normally I would punch back, but I don't want Tracy to notice me crying and tell Mom.

Blankly I stare out the window again. I start counting the cars that pass us. One . . . two . . . three. An ambulance with bright flashing lights pushes in front of us. Dad calmly eases on the brakes. Mom jerks her head up from dozing, then slowly drifts off again. Dad reassuringly puts his hand on her leg, then continues on, picking up speed. The ambulance triggers emotions in me, igniting my memory once again.

"Drew Monroe. M-O-N-R-O-E."

"Ah yes," the nurse booms, flipping through some papers. "Drew is being treated in Room 203. You may see him but please remain quiet. He's reported to be in very critical condition."

Our family nervously moves toward the elevator. Everyone smiles, as if they understand the torture our family is experiencing. Even the elevator purrs calmly, steadily rising. The doors open and push us out on the second floor.

A nauseating smell hits me hard, making me clench my stomach tight so it won't flip over. People busily scramble in all directions. We pass by halls and halls of rooms, all the same. From a nearby room, a man gasps and screams out in pain. I creep by, curiously stretching my neck inside the door. I can see many doctors surrounding a bed. But as I shift my weight to walk away, they break their huddle and pour into the hall.

They flit past me, leaving the room empty except for a barren figure covered by a clean white sheet. Everyone is seemingly unaffected, and the bustle continues as if nothing has ever happened.

Walking on, I count the floor tiles, praying that before I reach one hundred, the floor will swallow me up and place me back in a normal life. I look up and see the door, Room 203.

No one in my family says anything. Our shoulders sag, yet our muscles wait in tense anticipation. Our drooping bodies give a clear picture of our emotions.

We enter. A machine sadly beeps out his vital signs. There lies my brother. Tubes and wires connect in a maze of circuits all around him. A machine is helping him breathe and blood hangs from a bottle on the side, slowly dripping life into Drew's muscular arm. His face appears lifeless and rigid, not anything like the Drew that I know. I can't stand to look at my brother in this kind of shape. In tears, I turn toward the door. No one tries to stop me. They let me walk out of the quiet room and into the large corridor filled with bustling life. Dizzily, I stumble through the hallways until I find the entrance. Reaching the outdoor air, I sink down against the brick building, crying and crying for my brother Drew.

I never went back to the hospital again. I'd think

up excuses to stay home.

"I'm sorry, Drew, that I never came to see you, but I was scared, so scared," I whisper.

"What, Ben?" Dad breaks in. "I didn't hear what you said."

"Nothing, Dad. I was just talking to myself."

"Ok, son," he replies, and turns back to his driving, apparently satisfied with my answer.

I glance around at everyone in the car. It's hard to believe we're still together. It sure was difficult at home. Slouching back, I begin to doze again. My mind paints a picture of our house back in Landview. We'd stayed at home the rest of the summer to be near the hospital Drew was in. Yes, it sure was hard at home . . .

"Everyone ready to go see Drew?" Dad shouts from our front porch. I remain on the kitchen stool, polishing off my third bowl of Fruit Loops. Tracy joins Dad outside. She doesn't really understand what's going on, but is beginning to ask questions about why Drew is hurt and when he will be coming home. She can feel how sad our family is now, and she's becoming noticeably more irritable every day. Mom and Dad have been very lenient with her lately, too, which isn't helping her already-spoiled attitude.

"Carol, come on, we're leaving." Dad waits at the car door with Tracy hanging at his side.

Dad's been the strong, supportive one. Without him, I think we'd all drop instantly with nervous breakdowns.

"Ben, where's your mother? Aren't you coming with us?"

"I can't, Dad. Sorry, I've got things to do."

"Ben, I want you to come with us. Drew's your

brother; he needs you."

"He's in a coma! What does he know?" I yell angrily. Tears begin to well in my eyes. Immediately I regret what I said, seeing my father's hurt expression.

"Let Ben stay home," Mom whispers as she steps outside. Her eyes are puffy and bloodshot. She's changed so much since the accident. Usually her clothes are perfectly coordinated and her hair is carefully set, but now she appears ragged and worn. Yawning, she unconsciously pulls on Drew's summer jacket.

"Carol, that isn't your coat," Dad calmly states. His face is scrunched in concern. I know that he's worried about Mom as much as he is about Drew.

When Mom realizes whose coat it is, she breaks down in tears and rushes back to her room, slamming the door behind her. Lately all Mom ever does is lie in her room and cry. I worry so much about her.

Dad rushes after her, attempting to soothe her with gentle words. The two walk out hesitantly, arm-in-arm, to the car.

I place my dirty dishes in the overcrowded sink. Since Mom isn't doing any housework and Dad just doesn't seem to notice the terrible mess, our house has become a pit. I wade through the heaps of junk in the living room and hurry to my own room.

The car slows as we drive into a town, and I ease wearily back into reality.

"Hey, everyone, we're in Plainfield," Dad says, trying to sound enthused. "Only five more minutes to go."

No one answers him, although I think everyone heard. We pass by our friends' cottages. The car continues steadily past the beach at Scenic Lake. People wave to us and old familiar faces smile. Dad waves politely back, but Mom's face remains stone. She stares straight ahead as if we're on a dangerous mission.

Finally we arrive at our cottage. Everyone wearily steps out and picks up a suitcase to carry inside—everyone except me. I stiffly walk down to the dock. It seems like ages since we were here last. I wish we were back in Landview.

I glance up at our cottage. Tracy is at the study window, watching me. I frown, because the study brings back painful memories. We have a study exactly like it at home, and I think about the time Dad called me in for a talk. I think about how I sat swallowed up in Dad's leather couch, knowing it was important because we kids were never allowed in this study. I tried to recall having done something wrong that I would get in trouble for, but I couldn't think of anything bad or out of the ordinary.

Finally, Dad walked in. His head hung low and when his eyes met mine, I noticed that they were red and puffy.

"Ben, son, this is very hard for me to tell you, so please be patient." He wiped his eyes with an already-damp handkerchief. "Your brother was so good and I know you loved him just as we all loved him—very much. We've got to work together as a family to help each other through this tragedy, because we need you, Ben, and you need us." He could barely speak without choking. I'd never seen him act like this before.

"What is it, Dad?" I was so scared. I began to cry before he told me, because, of course, I already knew. He pulled me close and hugged me tight. My ribs ached and it was hard to breathe, but I clung to him even tighter, praying that what I had been thinking was wrong.

"Ben, Drew died early this morning."

Drew died early this morning . . . Drew died early this morning . . . The words echo through my head as I stop at the exact spot where Drew dove.

"Why did I have to throw the watch *there?*" I whisper. "If I hadn't done that, Drew would still be alive now." I begin to cry again, but this time I cry even harder and everything inside of me hurts. I kneel, my knees digging into the sharp corners of the dock which press deep marks into my skin. My head aches from the pressure and heat of the day. I feel as though every muscle is screaming for a whole night's rest without tossing and turning or reliving painful nightmares. But I hardly notice the physical pain; it's what I'm feeling in my heart that hurts the most.

Through the rotting cracks between the boards, I glance down to see the lake's clear bottom. The glint of steel catches my eye. The watch I'd carelessly thrown in for Drew still lies there, half-covered by sand. I wiggle out of my torn T-shirt and take off my shoes and socks. With only my shorts on, I slip into the cool water and lift the watch from the bottom. I pull it close to me, clasping it tightly with both hands as I surface for air. I pull myself back up onto the dock. The watch is still ticking and in good condition.

"Drew, I'm really going to miss you," I whisper, scraping off the loose sand covering the watch face. Slowly I wrap it up in my T-shirt, making sure it's secure.

Rising to my feet, I wipe the tears from my eyes. Fresh tears insistently seep back as I trudge up to our cottage, ready to help unpack again.

ABOUT THE AUTHOR

Jeanine Skendzel lives in Traverse City, Michigan, where she attends Traverse City Sr. High School. She enjoys athletics, particularly basketball, long-distance running, tennis, and skiing. She reports, "My second home is the gym." Miss Skendzel wrote "Summer's End" while in the ninth grade at Traverse City Jr. High School.

The View from Downstairs

by JOHN PETERS

As I stood on the corner waiting for the cars to pass, a sharp gust of winter air burned my face and reminded me to wear a scarf next time. I was behind my three friends, Vinnie, Alex, and Lance, who had run through traffic to get across the street. They weren't waiting for me, either.

After the final little import passed, I dashed across the street with my head down, trying to block the wind. Once on the other side, I put my hands in my pockets and jogged across the snow-covered park to catch up with the guys. The seventy-five cents in my right pocket began to jingle, inspiring me to hum the music to "Jingle Bells."

I was still humming as I caught up with the guys. They were talking about how stupid the movie we watched that night at Daphne's house was. It was an old story, a Disney film, about twin girls who meet for the first time at summer camp and switch places. I don't know why we watched it. I remembered seeing it in eighth grade at my girlfriend's babysitting job. That was two years ago.

Vinnie heard me humming and began to sing along. Only his version was a little different. "Jingle bells, Batman smells, Robin laid an egg, Batmobile lost its wheel and . . ."

Haw-haw-haws filled the air as all three of them doubled over. I stopped humming.

After the new joke became an old joke, Vinnie got a big grin on his face and said, "Eh, Lance, did you tell Diana you loved her tonight?"

"Yeah," Lance replied as if it were routine.

"Well, I told Erica I wanted to marry her," said Vinnie, with a little snicker. "She loved it. How 'bout you, Al?"

"We didn't do much talking," Alex said in his deep voice. After a few moments of trying to act macho, he began to laugh at his own joke. Alex was the youngest of us, but he'd been shaving since seventh grade. We were all sophomores, and just last week I asked Dad if I could borrow his razor for the first time.

I didn't say anything. The four of us had just spent the evening at Alex's girlfriend Daphne's house. We'd all been watching the movie, but within twenty-five minutes, Al, Vinnie, and Lance had disappeared with their girlfriends. Not me. Nicole and I watched the rest of the movie and then tried to name the Fifty Ways to Leave Your Lover. We had about fifteen when Nicole stopped.

"Jason, how come you haven't asked me to go upstairs with you?"

"Well," I muttered, "I just thought we could talk

and . . . well . . . um . . . I don't know. Do you . . . I
mean, if you want . . . I mean . . . I don't know."

She laughed and then dropped the subject.

I had never been a smooth talker with the ladies.
For me, a girlfriend was an occasional luxury. These
guys, on the other hand, considered them necessities.

Nicole and I met at Alphonso's Pizza Place two
weeks ago. She was with her three friends and I was
with mine. Vinnie took the liberty of introducing himself to the girls, who were sitting in the next booth.
Since there were four guys and four girls, we had to
"pair up." Nicole and I got along pretty well.

We talked about school and families and friends—
the usual small talk. Nicole was very good at keeping
conversation going. I constantly found myself with nothing to say, so to kill the monotony I would hum a song
to myself. Through this, we discovered that we had
the same musical tastes. The girls Vinnie, Alex, and
Lance hooked up with were gigglers. They thought
everything Vinnie said was hilarious. Nicole giggled,
but she giggled at good jokes. Lance's dirty jokes were
not her idea of humor. At the end of the night, I somehow managed to get Nicole's number, and the other
three guys arranged for all of us to meet at a later date.
I talked to Nicole a few times during the week and
saw a movie with her and the gang the following Saturday. Tonight was only my third time seeing her. I liked
Nicole because she had at least half a brain, which was
more than Lance's girl, Diana, had. I thought about
some of the things the guys said and wondered: Why
do girls fall for their phony lines? What makes girls
so dumb?

I was cold. My toes stung because I had holes in

the front of both my shoes. The wind was blowing so hard I had to squint to see where I was going. Alex told a dirty joke and everyone laughed. I could see the breath rise and disappear from their mouths. Even I laughed.

The forest preserve. I'd always hated having to go through Abigail Place Forest Preserve. I can remember when I was little and I used to walk home from Mersur School by myself. The forest preserve was a shortcut, but I never took it because I was chicken.

The reason I was chicken is a pretty strange story. My brother Eddie, who is three years older than me, once told me Santa Claus and the Easter Bunny lived in the forest preserve. Being only three at the time, I didn't know any better, and I had my brother take me there. Eddie led me along the path with a big smile on his face. He kept saying, "I hope you've been good, ha ha ha, or Santa will put coal in your stocking, and the Easter Bunny will give you one in the kisser with his carrot." Of course, I fell for it, and I even brought a cookie for each "celebrity." I held them both in my hand in the right pocket of my parka. We trudged along for a few minutes until we reached the middle of the forest preserve. There, on the little bench along the side of the path, two winos sat drinking. I guess I was staring because one of the winos yelled out, "Hey, you little kid! What are you lookin' at?" I looked up at my brother and his face was as pale as a new baseball. He wasn't moving, either. I started crying and ran back the way we came. Eddie came tearing by and passed me. Behind me, I could hear the sound of a bottle breaking. That night, safe at home, my brother told me of his big lie. I kicked him in the leg. In my hand were two smashed cookies covered with sweat. Ever since then, I've been afraid to enter the Abigail Place Forest Preserve.

The mouth to the pathway was pitch black. I could hardly even see the trees. To the right of the path I could see a sign which read Keep All Dogs On Leashes, but over the words someone had spray-painted in red a Nazi swastika. Chained to the sign was a metal garbage can. Scattered over the asphalt path were several broken bottles. The only sounds were those of our feet crunching the snow as we walked.

"Anyone want a cigarette?" Lance asked. I nodded my head and took a cigarette because I figured it would warm my body or at least my hand.

Vinnie and Alex had been smoking since eighth grade. They were the bullies at our school. They beat up everyone in the class, except Lance and me, to prove they were tough. They were, too. I guess after watching so much TV they figured that smoking went along with being tough guys. They never let their parents or any of the nuns at school know; they were strictly weekend smokers. It hadn't killed them yet, though. In eighth grade Alex was the star of the football and basketball teams. Vinnie didn't play sports.

As we plodded along, I slowed down from the group's pace to avoid any inquisitions about my evening. I couldn't understand why they told each other everything they did in their separate bedrooms. It was the same thing each weekend, only sometimes it had a different twist to it, like a different girl or a kind of bra hook which took ten minutes to unhook. I figured they just liked to hear each other brag.

The smell of wet wood crept up my nose. I looked

around and saw only the outlines of trees in the darkness. Under my foot I heard a stick crack. My mind traveled back to my childhood and an episode of "Lost in Space." In this episode, the ship crash-landed on a planet where the plants were human. Whenever they were broken or stepped on, they screamed. The family soon learned to treat the plants with care. I wondered if the stick underfoot felt any pain. If it did, why didn't it scream? I sighed and continued walking.

A wind in the top of the trees made a strange echoing sound, and I grew uncomfortable. I looked up to the trees, watching for someone or something that might be after me. I imagined myself walking along with Nicole when suddenly The Joker or The Penguin appeared and grabbed her. I chased him but his speed was much greater than mine.

I lost the image as I stumbled over a hard mound of snow. I dropped my cigarette, but I didn't mind— I hadn't even taken any puffs.

Now my hands began to shake, not just because of the cold, but because I felt all alone. Vinnie, Alex, and Lance were ahead, not even thinking about me. They were more concerned with their conquest of the world's entire sophomore female population. Even Lance hit it off with his girlfriend tonight. He said he'd told her he loved her. For some reason, I didn't think he was serious. Now I was the oddball. I was the only one who didn't go upstairs tonight. I was sure to get some heat for that, but I guess they just weren't like me. Or I wasn't like them. I wondered how long it would be before they decided I wasn't cool anymore.

Up in front of me the outlines of the three guys were all I could see. Alex's was the biggest. He had on his rugby jacket and it just made him look big. I glanced down at my tweed coat and decided I'd better button up. Vinnie's head appeared to be huge from the back. He hadn't gotten a haircut in a while. Lance dashed into the bushes and unzipped his pants.

I jogged up to the line of guys and heard Vinnie and Alex discussing their night's achievements. Lance finished his business in the woods and joined us.

"Hey, Jay, how was *your* evening?" Vinnie asked, as he turned his head toward me.

"Well, um, we just talked," I said casually, knowing that lying would get me nowhere. Lance got a big kick out of this and laughed until he turned dark pink.

"Shut up, Lance! I'm sorry Nicole isn't that type."

Alex, who apparently was laughing too, said, "We'll see about Nicole."

"Yeah, we'll see, Jay!" Lance said. "Hey, how'd your parents ever come up with a name like 'Jay'? Were they skimming the dictionary and when they hit 'J' they said 'here we go'?"

No, I thought. Actually my name is Jason. I was named after my dad's favorite TV character, Jason, of "Jason: The Intergalactic Space Traveler." I looked ahead of me and saw the opening to the forest preserve.

"Jay, how are things going with Nicole, anyway?" Vinnie asked with a strange smirk on his face. I got suspicious.

"What? Why? What did she say?"

"Well," Vinnie began slowly, "to tell ya the truth, you're about to get dumped. Nicole's about to go out with Ed Berkley."

"Who? That senior guy?"

"Yup. So I guess she is 'that type.'"

"Shut up, Vinnie."

"Go to hell, Jay."

I was enraged. They were lying about Nicole. Nicole wasn't the kind of girl who would let some creep like Berkley take advantage of her. Girls like that had absolutely no dignity. If Nicole went out with this senior guy, she would definitely become cheap. Who was this guy, anyhow? I was in total shock. She had *braces,* for crying out loud! I couldn't believe they'd think Nicole was that kind of girl! Or was she? I didn't know.

"You're a bunch of liars," I screamed.

"Go to hell, Jay," Vinnie repeated.

I exploded. "Vinnie, you're such a jerk! You all are! Haven't you ever thought about *anything?* Haven't you ever gotten up in the middle of the night and just thought about stuff?"

"Go to hell." He said it again. I couldn't believe it.

I ran. I ran through the snow out of the forest preserve and down the block. I didn't stop until I was out of breath. I looked back and saw them in the same place. Vinnie was laughing, Alex was lighting a fresh cigarette, and Lance was staring right at me. I started running again. I ran for a block and a half, thinking about nothing. My mind was so empty it hurt. I stopped and sat on a curb. I looked at my watch. Twelve o'clock. I had a half-hour to get home. My feet weren't cold anymore. They were just numb.

About the Author

John Peters lives in Evanston, Illinois, where he attends Evanston Township High School. His interests include lacrosse, Hacky Sack, writing, "and Marilyn Monroe." He wrote this story while in the tenth grade.

Frostee

by ROPER CLELAND

My ulcer was coming back. I could tell it was going to start bothering me when I became revolted at the sight of a melted Frostee on the wooden bench in the center of Crosscreek Mall.

It was when I was telling him I was leaving, leaving for good, so I was tracing the grain of the wood on the bench over and over to keep from crying.

I knew it wouldn't be pleasant. Nothing in my life was pleasant, yet I enjoyed the feeling. I enjoyed the way it felt to drop the verbal bomb in the "popular" section of Musicland while we were looking at a wonderfully wretched Dinosaur Jr. album. And I enjoy the way it feels to say I have fallen in with the wrong crowd this past year. I know it conjures up the romantic image of black leather jackets, but in truth they are just sweet, bitchy kids with very twisted lives, and the only problem is that they twisted my life, too, so that I was pulled down with them, even if I didn't drink, or smoke their pot. They gave me their hell anyway, so that I hate food but crave it, yet at the same time love seeing my bones become more clear through my skin, until I don't know if it's natural or if I'm anorexic. But that is the least of my problems, now that my hero has gone off to college.

"Never returning," he swore to me in his darkened room, not realizing that now I have to leave, too.

My life had taken a nosedive into pits of tar, so that I stared at the puddle of strawberry Frostee, telling the boy things that made him cry out of his pain, our pain, my pain. Only the pain was exquisitely beautiful. There was pleasure in having my stomach rumble in emptiness as I blindly attempted to empty my life of love. It was making him call me sick in the same breath that he was saying he would always love me.

My parents talk of sending me to a psychiatrist, who will believe the ulcer is all in my imagination. But if you think about it, most of my problems could be imagined. I always did have a good imagination—even in sixth grade I believed in faeries, and I still, in my not-a-child-but-definitely-not-an-adult stage, have unreal friends.

I make them up with my wrong-crowd best friend, so that we can freak people out in the same way that I laugh because my reputation has fallen to pieces, without me even doing anything to smash it. For some reason I think it is funny to have people believe I am a druggie and a bisexual, so that when I was on the hard mall bench, tied in my own personal hell, my childhood best friend—who believed in faeries with me—passed by without even smiling. She was dressed in country-club white—the color my hero Dante despised—but I guess that doesn't matter now.

He left us to find "freedom." Left me alone and missing him. I miss our shared makeup and midnight food orgies, but I don't eat anymore, so that doesn't matter, either.

Nothing matters. I promised I'd leave, promised I'd leave everyone I cared for behind, which the boy couldn't understand as I tried to explain in that damned mall while my stomach raged and I enjoyed the dramatic feeling of the imagined movie camera behind me, recording my life.

I never let people open car doors for me. Dante didn't, and he warned me of guys who did. Boys who open them just want to get you in the back seat that much sooner, he explained. But I let him open it that night at the mall; I guess I was too tired to protest. I mean, it wasn't exactly like he was in the mood to mess around.

I felt like I was betraying Dante to surrender my feminism to a car door. Then again, I was losing so many of our shared beliefs now that he was gone. Without him, they seemed to dissolve with the rest of my cheery life.

Dante was the first one to notice my eating problems. He would fix me milk shakes and soothe me into drinking them like no one else could. When someone called me and he answered the phone, he would not give it to me unless I had eaten all the appropriate meals of that day.

He left behind his eyeliner. It was a cheap drugstore kind that he hid deep in his medicine cabinet so my mom would not find it. He'd put it on after he went out and would wash it off before he came back in. For a while there, Mom thought he had gotten into drugs because she always saw him with red eyes.

I used that same eyeliner the night of the mall and melted Frostee. I dressed up nice to tell him my news, to look good for my pretend movie camera, dressed up in what I felt was dramatically appropriate. Black clothes, black mascara and white face powder, even black toenail polish, which he called punk through his tears.

It didn't bother me as it once would have, and the thought made me want to cry even more, the thought that he didn't affect me. But I merely traced the fake wood grain with the tip of my fingernail, not painted black because painted nails only look good on weird guys like Robert Smith. I just could not let that wretched mascara and eyeliner run.

I have never worn eyeliner since. I threw Dante's old Cover Girl stuff away, along with the ritzy Estée Lauder Mom bought me (since she believes nice girls wear nice makeup and nice boys don't wear makeup at all). But she really does love Dante, as much as I loved him, as much as I loved the boy on the mall bench, as much as I loved to hate the painfully stark world I was creating.

Not even her own son, and Mom loved him. He only lived with us since the start of high school, when his parents kicked him out of the house, but he was family all the same. Mom and Dad are loaning him money for college. I called him my brother because he was more brother to me than any real one could have been. It's not like I stick to reality all that much, so if he's brother in my mind, that's the way it is.

I was younger by two years. I just wasn't expecting him to graduate a year early and slam out of my life so soon. I thought he wouldn't do that to me. I was the one who offered him a home. I was the one who spent surreal nights with him, reading poetry in Aisle 4 of FoodMax at 3 A.M.

We got up and walked to the bookstore that night at the mall—humor section, like some sick joke. I flipped through Calvin and Hobbes but did not even see the pictures; I mumbled about our old trips to the bookstore; I mumbled things about Dante that the boy did not want to hear. But what I had already said was worse. What else did he want me to do now? Run into his arms apologizing? That would just not do—apologies don't cover up such big gashes, and anyway, I would have slipped and fallen on my face into the wet Frostee. I knew I would, in the same way I always get the giggles during the most serious parts of lectures.

Then he said something that tore my insides in two, which might have been good, since I hadn't felt true emotions in a while. He whispered the truth: that I cared more for Dante than anyone else. More than a teenage crush. More than our relationship, which he did not think of as a teenage crush, and thought I did not think of as a teenage crush until the way I was treating him now.

The irony of the joke books around me was too much to bear. I took his hand and led him out, silently. He drew back as we emerged, blinking, from the store. It was the first time he had ever drawn back from me. We always seemed to naturally touch. It never intentionally happened, but it was like we flowed together, so much so that a lot of people thought we had sex. (But Dante told me not to lose my virginity until I was positive it was the right person, so, of course, it was all a rumor.)

They thought Dante and I had sex, too, or some craziness like that, probably because around here no one can imagine two people of the opposite sex having a non-lustful relationship. Truthfully, we did go out for a little while. He was my first boyfriend, my first kiss, my first eye-opener to individuality. That's what I began to think about at the mall, scuffing through Belk's, wondering if breaking the silence would make it harder or easier.

It must have bothered the boy to never have my complete attention. I saw the truth that strawberry-Frostee night. I knew it would hurt him, but it was too late to change it, and who's to say I would have changed it if I could?

When his flight to New England was called, I smiled. I didn't want to show him how much I cared, since he didn't want to have to deal with little sisters bawling on his path to freedom, and I didn't want to show Mom how Dante had hurt me in the end, after she had warned me the first time she met him that he would only end up hurting me. She was crying herself.

I told him to have a great rest of his life. Then a flight attendant interrupted us and there it was, the end. It was so undramatic I didn't realize it had happened until his plane swooped off the runway, carrying him to his goals and me to my misery.

I slept on the way back. Tired because I hadn't eaten much. Tired because lately all my life had been was sleeping. Sleeping, wasting time until I could sleep again, wasting time by not eating, wasting time by sneaking out to a keg party and letting my hair fill up with the perfume of cigarette smoke, wasting time by hurting myself and watching my own reactions. Sleep and warmth were all I could think about. I froze all day at school inside the icy buildings, then stretched out under the sun at lunch, my whole body searching for warmth. I would greedily take it in, more and more, until I was so hot I got dizzy. I could not eat my peanut butter and jelly sandwich on whole wheat bread and was too tired to argue with my friends about Dante, who had taken to a different crowd and was called a snob by this one because he didn't drink, didn't smoke, didn't even have the weakness to let them suck him down like I allowed them to do to me.

He said it was the end on our circling path through Belk's—not my hero with me, but my boyfriend, the earth beneath my feet. Wait, I finally thought. That can't be. The end has already come, and there cannot be two ends, can there?

"No," I told him, "this is merely the beginning."

"Beginning of what?" he asked, made slightly sarcastic by the pain. "The end?"

"No," I said again. "No, the beginning of the rest of my life." The old cliché had slipped out between makeup counters.

"The rest of your life will not be here," he said bitterly. "You mean the rest of your life that you start by leaving me in the exact way Dante left you—it's a vicious cycle, you know."

I really looked at him for the first time that night, since there was no wood grain around. I had to find the grain of his face instead. I followed the flesh of his expression, and suddenly I felt relieved. I wanted to laugh, to hug him and dance silly steps the way we used to, to try on old-lady shoes like Dante and I once did. I wanted to cry wildly, to curl up on the dirty cream linoleum and sob. The relief brought back all the emotions I hadn't felt in so long over the rumble of my stomach.

But words are powerful. Everyone had told me this, and I had never believed it until now. Too much had been said by my own wretched tongue to softly touch him and apologize. I didn't care, though. I cared only that I was beginning to feel things. I finally felt bad for causing him pain.

The invisible movie camera was at my back, prompting me to take action. I told him he had every reason to dump me if he wanted, even if I had decided I wouldn't leave for at least another year. I needed to straighten things out and mature a little before I traipsed into the world on my own.

He didn't pull me into his arms or say he loved me. No, he only said something pretty obvious. He said things would be different from now on. He was looking at me for the first time that night. Perhaps tracing the flesh of my face, too.

I laughed at the mannequins that looked like they were frozen into position moments before being hit by a train. I laughed because I knew in the future there would be a lot of times I would not feel like laughing, considering the work I had before me. I laughed because things would be different and I would be the one responsible for shaping how it turned out.

A girl went up to the makeup counter and asked if they carried Cover Girl. Dante had made the same mistake once. He told the saleslady he had worn makeup since he was twelve, which was a total lie, but her expression had been funny.

"Come on," I told the boy after my strange laughing fit. "I need to buy some eyeliner to send Dante. He forgot his, and heaven knows he doesn't know which kind to buy himself."

I put a hand to my stomach, wondering if a little food might make the pang go away.

ABOUT THE AUTHOR

Roper Cleland attends Greenwood High School in her hometown of Greenwood, South Carolina. She wrote this story while in the ninth grade at Northside Jr. High School. Writing is her main interest, but she also loves to travel, draw, and play the guitar.

Kenston High School
17425 Snyder Road
Chagrin Falls, OH 44023-2728

The Ultimatum

by KRIS REICH

T he bell rang, interrupting my pleasant daydreams. John quickly hit me on the shoulder and told me that we were going to be late for the bus. I struggled out of my chair and ran for the door, which was filled with a mob of eighth-, ninth-, and tenth-graders. On our way to my locker I saw Erik. As soon as I spotted him, I looked at the floor.

"What a loser," John mumbled. Erik turned around in disgust.

John saw me looking at the ground. "What's the matter?" he asked.

"Nothing," I lied. Erik had always been a friend of mine, but times had changed. Now I wouldn't be caught dead with him in public.

With that, John and I proceeded to the bus. We sat in the back, where our gang was harassing a little fifth-grader. He started to cry so we left him alone. Then we talked about losers in our grade. Erik was soon brought up in the conversation.

"Erik is such a fat loser," John said.

"Lay off Erik, you hardly know him."

"I think Peter may have the hots for Erik. Are you one of those types?" joked one member of the gang.

"Shut up!" I replied.

The gang and I did not talk for the rest of the bus ride. Soon John and the rest of the gang got off, and Erik and I were the only ones left. I moved to the front seat and sat down next to him.

"How's life?" I asked.

"None of your business."

"I know you must be a little mad, but I tried to stick up for you when they started harassing you."

The bus pulled up to a screeching stop, and we got off.

"Some friend you are. You're embarrassed to speak with me in the halls for fear of wrecking your reputation. You're a damn snob!"

Without thinking, I drew back my hand and swung hard at his nose. The blow sent him stumbling into the snowbank.

I looked at him and at the blood all over the snowbank. I gave a little chuckle, for form's sake, and ran toward my house.

I got to my driveway; I could already hear the screams from the house. My legs were tired, and I was breathing so hard it could be heard next door.

When I opened the door, the fighting ceased. My dad was the first to talk. "Oh, great, our darling boy is here. He gives so much devotion and love to his parents. The minute he gets home he parades up to his room."

"I'm just sick of all your damn fighting all the time."

"When I get through with you, you're going to wish you were never alive."

This time my mother cut in: "If you lay one hand on my boy, we're going to leave."

"You just stay out of this."

I waited until the fight was back in full swing and they didn't even know I was in the room. Then I slipped upstairs.

When I got to my room, I quickly turned on my radio to drown out the screams of the fight. I was getting used to the fighting, but it still made me sick to hear them.

I was up in my room thinking of excuses not to do my homework. Then I thought of the problem with Erik. He was a loser. If a loser had talked to John like that, John would have killed him.

Then my concentration was broken by a vigorous knock at my bedroom door. It was John. I invited him in.

"Do your parents always fight like this?"

"No, it just started a week ago when my dad was fired."

"I heard what you did to Erik."

"He deserved it. Why should I let him talk to me like that?"

"What I came over for is to ask you why you even talk to that scum Erik."

"I guess it's a change from being a loser to being popular." There was a bad crash of a chair downstairs, and I turned up my radio louder.

"You know, if you were to hit me or any other member of the gang, you would be in the hospital right now."

"Well, I didn't, so get off my case." I wanted to take back what I said, but he cut me off.

"You better watch how you talk to me." He left, and the door slammed hard behind him.

I couldn't understand John. Why didn't he hit me?

That night I lay in bed thinking over the bad things. I thought back to when I had gotten an F on my history test. I thought about my parents. Then the problem with Erik arose. Was it all right to hit him? Why didn't John hit me? If only I could take that back, I would have never hit Erik. Finally, I went to sleep.

I got up the next morning dreading the coming praise for hitting Erik, when praise wasn't necessary from my point of view. At 7:30 A.M. I headed for the bus. I saw Erik sitting in the front of the bus by himself. I had half a mind to stop and apologize, but John and the gang approached me.

"The gang and I were talking, and we decided that you have to choose—Erik or us! Because this could damage our reputation as well as *ruin* yours," said John.

I looked at Erik, then back at John.

The answer must have been written all over my face, because John reached out his hand and said, "Welcome back."

ABOUT THE AUTHOR

Kris Reich lives in Chagrin Falls, Ohio, and attends the eighth grade at Hawken School in Lyndhurst. He enjoys sailing, tennis, skiing, and swimming.

A Start

by ELIZABETH BUHOT

He unfolds his arms, exposing his body to the chill mountain air. Grass lies silently beneath his naked feet. Alone, he slips into the dewy growth, finding a place among the weeds. His limbs lie like pale, limp tendrils as he sits, motionless. Only his mind is stirring; it's thinking, I'll just lie here and waste away. No one will know the difference.

A dog's deep bark cuts the air. Tobey bounds over, followed by his faithful master, Bub. "What's dat?" Bub says. "Whatdja find? Treasure?" No, not treasure, Jake thinks to himself. Get away from me, stupid dog.

As if he had heard, Tobey runs back to Bub's heels.

"Why, no, it's Mr. Jacob. Yes, indeed," Bub says, petting the dog's head. "Jake, whatcha doin', huh? Didja fall?" He sets down his metal detector. Jake nods; no words will come. He nods as he did when he was young and scared of people, even old backwoodsmen like Bub.

Bub bends closer to him, grinning through broken teeth. "Looks what I just found! Perty, huh? Givin' it to Willa tonight." He dangles an object over Jake's nose. Jake nods again, squinting to focus on the object. He is thinking of Willa, who is buried nearby in Bub's backyard. He thinks of Willa when she was alive, Willa who was there for everyone in these hills. Sixteen years ago, she was there for his mother, to boil water and get clean towels. She was there to cut her from her crying, screaming, bloody baby boy. If only she hadn't been . . .

The object is clear now; Jake puts his face in the grass. It's the ring he had bought for Abbey. "Gets you up," Bub says, extending his hand to Jacob. "It's gettin' late 'n' Miss Abbey'll be here soon to fetch ya fer school. Gets you on home 'n' gets you dressed!"

The problem, Jake thinks, is Abbey Smallman, his ex-best friend; she isn't coming to "fetch" him, not today or any day. Yesterday, she'd done her hair in puffy curls. Platinum strands rose from her head like steam. She is so far away now, he thinks. He thought of the times when he was small and reached for a steaming kettle from the stove, a kettle that was way up high. Willa would slap his hand and say "NO!" He would cry. He's crying now; this time it is Abbey who has slapped him.

Yesterday, she'd walked apart from him the whole way home. She paced him up the hill, walking backwards in front of him. Explaining with "uhs" and "wells" and "you knows," she told him she wouldn't walk the back way to school anymore. She'd walk on the main road now, not even so much as pausing at the foot of the path that led to his two-room cabin. "I am to walk straight to school without stopping; and I am to walk on the main road," she said plainly, "for Daddy says there's rabid coons running about now." Bub waddles down the path; Jake gets up.

How stupid does she think I am? he asks himself. She's out of reach now, and there's nothing I can do. Jake had heard about Abbey's "Coming Out" party— her introduction to kids from Westover and other town schools. He was pretty sure "Coming Out" meant moving out, leaving the hill people behind. He now knows it means she will follow in her sister's footsteps: graduate, go to college, marry some doctor. Jake feels foolish; there is no place for him in this picture. "Hell to whoever said you should marry your best friend," he says aloud, opening the cabin door. A bowl of oatmeal sits on the table in the front room. He sits down, checking the underside of the bowl, hopeful. Oh, give it up! he thinks to himself. His mother stopped leaving those notes long ago, the ones that said "Smile," or "Have a nice day." She'd long given up on attempts to communicate with her son. She'd serve him dinner or pack his lunches with as few words as possible. He wonders if that's how it is where she works; he wonders if she gives words to Abbey when she serves her breakfast.

He winces at the thought of his mother as his servant. Pushing away his bowl, he thinks of the story "Goldilocks." He begins to feel like he's stealing from her. What has he ever offered her? I don't deserve this, he thinks, even if the oatmeal is lumpy and cold.

He retreats to the garage, his bedroom. The cabin has one real bedroom, which is his mother's; when he was younger, they'd shared the room. Then, a few years ago, he'd taken all his things into the garage. It was a small lean-to on the side of the house which was never used since they had no car. Though it was rather cold, it was his own. His mother never said a word about the move, though a few weeks later the room was separated by a makeshift wall—a blanket hung over a clothesline. Days after that, a kerosene heater appeared on the floor. Since then, his mother had never set foot in his room.

After washing, she'd fold his clothes neatly and set them at the foot of his door. Now, he stoops down to find two "new" shirts. He knows they came from the box. Each month a box of clothes, food and toiletries would arrive at their door. When he was very young, he was told the box was from his father. "Where is my daddy?" he would ask.

His mother would swallow and answer, "Away at the war; your daddy's a big hero in Korea." As he grew, the war ended; by age ten, Jacob realized there was no father. At least, there was no "Daddy." His real father had given him nothing, not even a name. Jake took his mother's last name—MacAbbot.

The truth of the matter was that the box was sent in from the church in town. It was charity, and Jacob found out the hard way. One day, as the children were playing in the schoolyard, Georgie Smith grabbed him by his collar. He held Jacob up in front of the children and yelled, "Chicken Legs here's got MY shirt on! My mom gave away all my shrimp clothes—I wore this when I was FOUR."

A chorus of laughter followed as Jacob ran inside the school. Behind him he could hear Abbey scream, "Just you shut up, Georgie Smith, or would you like

a nice big knuckle sandwich?" He had looked back to
see her standing in her ruffly dress and pinafore, shaking her fist at the boys. Of course, everyone laughed
at her, too, but things like that never seemed to bother
Abbey.

As he slips the shirt on his back, he tries to put her
out of his mind. We aren't in second grade anymore,
he says to himself. Things are different. Why can't I
pull this together? he wonders, as his numb fingers
fumble over the buttons. His chest is blotchy from the
coldness by now. He kicks at the space heater, but hits
his foot on the corner of the bed. Clumsy jerk, you'll
never grow out of it! Everyone said his awkwardness
was "just a stage," and up until recently, he believed
it. Yesterday blew the little confidence he had.

It was as if Abbey had planted a small seed—rejection—in him. He was a sidewalk and the seed was
growing into a weed. It maneuvered through the faults,
his faults, and began to take over. Now it had twined
through his body, entangling him. It sucked all hope
and optimism from him.

He gives up on the buttons and grabs a blanket
from his bed. Ignoring the stench of kerosene, he lies
in front of the heater, wrapped in the blanket. Forget
about school, he thinks; I can't take it, not today. He
looks around the room for a moment. I may not see
this again, he thinks to himself, spying the half-packed
suitcase in the corner.

The suitcase had been lying there for weeks, ever
since he got the idea of going to Newhalf to mine coal.
It'll be hard, he thinks, but at least I'll be supporting
myself. Nobody here needs me anyhow. It'd be a bur-
den off Mom's back if I left. I'd be gone and she'd

have the place to herself and no one to worry about.

It bothers him that his mother'd never had a life of her own. He was even with her, inside her body, when she left home—she'd never been alone. Thrown from her home for getting pregnant at age sixteen, she sought refuge in this small West Virginia town, but found it merciless. The post office refused to hire her when she lied about her age; she was once caught stealing milk to feed her baby. A single mother, she was a social leper, received by the townspeople only as cheap labor.

Lately, Jacob tried to become as invisible as possible, but he always seemed to get in her way. In the mines, I won't be in the way of anyone, he thinks. I'll be deep underground and out of sight. And he has a small, small fear that if he doesn't leave soon, he'll never get out of this town; he'll never escape the worn, tired Appalachians. Without Abbey, he has no reason to stay.

He yawns and closes his eyes. They feel heavy inside his head; he hadn't slept much the night before. I'm leaving tonight, he resolves, and drifts off to sleep.

He wakes up feeling as though he's covered with mildew; it is late afternoon. His face is flushed and sweaty from sleeping in front of the heater. Damp hair clings to the back of his neck; his mouth is dry, but laced with an acidic taste. He decides to take a shower, but changes his mind as his feet feel the cold floor. He knows he'll cool off quickly.

He throws some more things into the suitcase. If I'm leaving tonight, I may as well do something for her. Entering the cabin's front room, he eyes the spotlessness. There's nothing I can do, he thinks. While most poor folks give up on cleanliness, his mother, a maid, always kept the house neat and clean. Every spring she'd launder the dingy curtains and throw rugs to make them as close to white as possible. The cupboards, no matter how bare, were always kept in order. I could check her room, he thinks. He hadn't been in there in years, and he wouldn't feel quite right entering now. He considers: she spends so much time in there lately, it must be clean. What else could she be doing but cleaning? She never reads or knits as she used to. Of course, she may not have the energy to do those things. She comes home awfully late these days. His hand reaches for the doorknob, but stops. I'll cook instead, he thinks.

He opens the cupboard, looking around. He considers the stuffing mix that came in last month's box, but opts for the rice instead. I'd better cook something cheap, he thinks; I'll probably burn it.

He has never cooked before. Gee, he thinks, if I stick around school till next year, I can take home economics. But inside, he knows he can't face school anymore; Abbey was the only friend he'd had. He couldn't very well consider HER a friend now; she even refused to walk with him. I am beneath her now, he thinks. Maybe she's forbidden to even SPEAK to me . . .

Getting a pan, he fills it with water from the stationary tub. As he walks across the room to the stove, the pan slips from his hand. I'm more trouble than I'm worth, he thinks, fetching the rag. He drops to his knees and mops up the spill. Just then, his mother walks in.

She stands tall, despite her weariness. Her eyes are

gentle, but her face is stern. It conveys a homegrown pride; it masks pain—never crying or frowning. She carries a brown paper bag in her hand. Turning to shut the door behind her, she notices her son is on the floor; he continues to wipe up the water. "Oh, there you are. Look at this," she says, attempting to disguise her fatigue with thin cheer. "Leftover chicken from the Smallmans. Oh, but I see you've got the rice out; would you rather have that?" Not waiting for an answer, she offers, "I'll make both. You must be starving; it's getting late. I'll try to hurry."

He looks up at her as she scurries around the kitchen, grabbing pots, running water, turning knobs. "I'm not hungry," he says, rising. He grabs a piece of bread from the counter and runs to his room. Lying on his bed, he picks at the bread, piece by piece. How am I going to tell her? he wonders. *Am* I going to tell her? A flash comes to his mind—paper. I'll write a note, he plans, and leave it on the table. I can go after she's asleep, and walk to town. Then I'll hitch a ride to Newhalf from a trucker.

Sitting for what seems like hours, he attempts to write the note. He writes "Dear Mom," but scratches out the "Dear." He then scratches out "Mom," thinking: Who else would I be writing to? He hears a knock at the door. Reluctantly, he rises to answer it. I told her I didn't want any dinner, he says to himself.

His mother stands in the doorway, her chest heaving with grief and frustration. Her eyes, squinted shut, are covered in creamy blue makeup which has started to run down her cheeks. "I . . . I . . ." she stammers.

He places his hands on her shoulders. "Are you all right?" he asks, frightened. "Should I fetch a doctor?"

She shakes her head from side to side. "N . . . N . . ." she says, sputtering.

"No. OK," he says, trying to keep calm. He has never seen her cry before, not even when Willa died. She must be hurt or something. "Calm down, calm down," he says.

She places one hand on the doorway, bracing herself. The other lies on her chest; the gasps subside into steady, deep breaths. He backs away and watches her. Something is odd. It's her dress; she's taken off the uniform. Where did that thing come from? This certainly isn't a nightgown; it's a homemade dress. The dress is a deep red and sags on her shoulders. Yet it is pinched at the hip and a fresh rip tears at the side. Little fringes of frayed fabric stick out into the air. She wears lipstick the color of the dress; traces of it, several shades lighter, are smeared beyond the corner of her mouth.

"What's the matter?" he wonders aloud, thinking, Boy, this is the most we've talked in a long time.

"The . . . the brush," she says, pulling at her hair. He maneuvers around her to find an ancient brush stuck to the side of her head. For lack of a curling iron, his mother had tried using a round brush to style her hair and it had gotten lost in her thick tresses.

"Need help?" he asks. She nods silently, looking at the floor. "Lemme get into the light," he says, pulling her under the light bulb. He unwraps one clump from the brush as split ends snap and fall to the floor. Then he pulls out another clump. "Ouch," she says, touching the spot where the hair was pulled from her scalp.

"Sorry," he says, trying to unravel another clump.

"Cut it," she says. "It'll take forever to unwrap it.

Just cut it."

"What?" he asks.

"Just cut my hair. Cut the brush out, OK?" she says.

"Whatever," Jake says gently, pushing past her to find the scissors.

She sits as he weeds through the cupboards. After a few minutes, she mutters, "The one on the far right. Top shelf."

He stands, studying the complicated pattern of hair wrapped in the brush. "What are you waiting for?" she asks, tapping her foot.

"Um, uh, I don't know what to do," he says.

"Just cut," she says. "Cut straight across right before where the hair meets the brush."

He takes the scissors and carefully snips. I'm going to mess this up, he thinks, I really am going to screw it up. Each time a lock falls to the ground, he winces.

Finished, he stands back to look at his work. "All done?" she asks, standing.

"Yep," he says. She goes to the mirror to check her hair. Standing behind her, he can see her reflection grimace. A large patch of hair on the right side is a half-foot shorter than the rest.

"Uh, you won't be able to tell when you put it in a bun for work . . ." he says.

She walks toward the chair. "Ah, what the heck," she says. "Finish it off."

Shrugging, he picks up the scissors. "Would you like it washed first, ma'am?" he asks, pretending he is a stylist. He tries hard to keep a comfortable distance.

A hurt look spreads over her face. "I just did," she says, sitting.

He stands behind her and begins to cut. Surveying her head, he thinks to himself: This'll take a while. I'd better talk. But what will I say? Only clichés occur. "All dressed up and no place to go?" he asks.

"I had plans," she says.

"The Smallmans having a dinner party or something?" he asks. No answer. "I'd better get you done quick then, I guess."

"Really," she says.

"Huh?" he asks.

"Is that all you think I do? Work, work, work?"

"Well, where ARE you going, then?" he asks.

"I am . . ." she says, "or I WAS, going to the Fall Festival."

"Really," he says in disbelief. "Who's your date?"

"No one you know," she answers stiffly. He knew what that meant: it meant that she didn't have a date. I'd better change the subject, he thinks.

As he thinks about what to say, he looks at her face. She is pretty, he thinks. I don't take after her at all. Yet there is something worn about her; she looks older than thirty-two. He spots gray in one auburn strand as he clips. It's probably my fault, he thinks. I could've helped out more, I could have . . . Well, I could have done something for her! "So did you make that dress yourself?" he asks.

"Yes," she answers. "Do you like it?"

He doesn't. "Yes," he answers.

"Got the fabric in town," she says proudly.

"Really?" he says. Funny, he thinks; this isn't like talking to a mother at all. This is how the barber talks to me. "Should I hurry?" he asks. "So you won't be late?"

"I'm not . . . I can't . . . I can't go," she says.

"Why not?" he asks.

"I've . . . I've never been there before and . . ." she says, her voice faltering.

The clichés come again. "There's a first time for everything," he says.

"Really," she says, "it was a stupid idea. I don't know those people; I don't know what to say to them, or how to act with them."

Jake watches a wisp fall to the ground as he thinks about her words. He stops cutting for a moment, remembering the time Abbey had taken him to a party in town. He'd sat in the corner all evening. It was obvious he wasn't known or wanted there. "I know what you mean," he says, and continues to cut.

"I just feel like there's nobody I know here. I see 'em every day, at the grocer's or somewhere, but they all pretend like they don't see me."

"Exactly," Jacob says.

"And when Willa died," she continues, "that was just the worst. She was the last person I could really—"

"Talk to," he says, thinking of Abbey. At least Abbey isn't dead, he says to himself.

"Yes," she says quietly. "I feel lonely now, Jacob."

He nods; he is beginning to understand. "Mom?" he asks, hesitant because he doesn't know if the question is appropriate.

"Yes?"

"So why did you want to go to the festival?"

She pauses, staring straight ahead. "Well, it had to do with being lonely. Me being lonely, and . . . and you being lonely too, I guess."

"What do you mean?" he asks, trying to be casual.

"Jake, Jake, Jake," she sighs. "You really don't think

much of me, do you?" He opens his mouth to say, "Of course I do," but she continues. "I've been watching you. I can tell when something's wrong."

"I'm fine," he says. The last thing I need to do is give her trouble, he thinks. Besides, she wouldn't understand.

"See, you don't want to admit that your old lady knows something . . . but I know something's up. Now, I may not know what it is," she says, laughing hoarsely, "but I know THAT it is. So I thought maybe having a man in your life would kind of help you out a little, you know?" As she speaks she gestures casually with her hands, trying to overcome the heaviness of the topic.

He looks down sadly as he evens the back ends of her hair. He wanted a dad, but he didn't want her to become a wife. That would take away the little freedom she has left. If she could get a good man, a gentle man, he thought . . . but not at her age, not in this town. Though she was pretty, the townsmen would only take her as a second wife, someone to look after the kids now that their mother had died or been divorced. They would marry her as a workhorse.

"What do you think?" she asks.

"I think there are plenty of men who'd be happy—"

"I mean," she says, "do you want a pa?"

"Do you want a husband?" he asks.

She pauses. "Well, really," she says, "I could take it or leave it. Ya know, once you're used to your freedom, marriage is kind of scary. Besides, I kind of like making it on my own," she laughs. "If you call this making it."

He thinks about these views on marriage and begins to see something new. When he proposed to Abbey, he didn't realize marriage might scare her, take away her freedom—or his! Maybe that's why . . . well, so what? Just because she won't marry me doesn't mean she hates me. If I could just talk to her, he thinks. His insides begin to feel hollow. He is still crushed by her flat rejection; he still wants to hide. I've got to tell Mom.

"I'd kind of like to make it on my own, too," he says.

She rises to look in the mirror. "It's so short," she says. Suddenly, she turns around. "What do you mean you'd like it on your own? You're not . . ." She cannot finish her sentence.

Hundreds of thoughts go through his head; for a moment, he forgets about himself. He looks at her torn dress, then at the brush on the table, webbed with hair. He thinks back to when she appeared at the door; now it seems long ago. He recalls her helplessness. That terror remains in her eyes now, and Jacob sees this. "No," he answers, "I'm not leaving."

That look disappears from her eyes and she sighs. "Good, you had me worried there. I mean, of course someday you'll make it just fine, but at sixteen . . . Well, I of all people should know—it's tough." She looks around the room, avoiding his gaze. She picks up the brush, tapping it on the table. Finally, she looks at him. "Besides, if you leave, I'd have to get a car or something for the garage, and I . . ."

He sees that she isn't making any sense, but he knows what she means. "I need you too, Mom," he says. He looks at her: she looks as if she is about to cry, but she smiles. "Now I've got some unpacking to do," he says.

"Need help?" she offers.

"No, I can handle it," he says.

He's alone in the garage once again. Only now, a smile plays at the corners of his mouth. As he sees his schoolbooks, the smile disappears. You know what this means, he thinks to himself: two more long years of school. He can't bear the thought of going back to school—the humiliation. He feels betrayed; he feels that Abbey has joined the crowd that has taunted and embarrassed him since the first grade. But something inside him wants to make up with her, to become friends again. As he removes the last shirt from the suitcase, it hits him: Even though Abbey doesn't need me, I guess someone here does. It's a start . . .

ABOUT THE AUTHOR

Elizabeth Buhot lives in Pittsburgh, Pennsylvania, where she attends the Ellis School. She wrote this story while in the tenth grade. Miss Buhot writes for her school newspaper and heads Youth Cry, a student group committed to environmental health and healing. Whenever possible, she likes to attend alternative rock concerts or go swimming.

Sing Softly, Wind

by DIANE MATOUS

I strained against the cool steel faucet handle. It pressed into my palm for a second, then gave way. The water gushed out into the black latex bucket, a foam of tiny droplets spraying upward as it hit bottom.

"I'm leaving!" I heard my brother's voice calling from the back of the barn, and the dull scrape and thud as he shut the heavy oak door on Calypso's stall. The moths fluttering around the uncovered light bulb cast eerie shadows on everything.

"Wait a minute, Anthony," I pleaded, unwilling to admit my fear. "I'm almost done."

"I'm sick of staying out late!" he complained, but I knew he would linger a little longer. He, too, knew what it was to feel the fear of the night. Ever since we were very small and had explored the woods and fields together, we had known that fear, a primitive, ancient fear wrought from the days when our ancestors crouched noiselessly as the first threads of darkness gathered. It was a fear of the silent things that hunt by dark, that cannot be sensed until there is no time to run.

The pitch of the gurgling water rose as the bucket filled. I shut off the water before it had a chance to overflow onto the clean dry straw, put there to absorb previous such accidents. My pony rumbled loudly.

"Coming, Ginger! Hold your horses," I laughed. I picked up the bucket, rather heavy now, and carried it to her stall, staggering a little to counterbalance its weight. I lifted it over the fence, bumping the bottom on the top beam and sloshing water onto my jeans and into my shoes. It was ice-cold and I made a futile effort to shake it out. Ginger came over and pushed her pretty bay head into the bucket as I hooked it to the holding clip.

"Thirsty, huh, girl?" I spoke softly, reaching over to rub her forehead. She lifted her head and looked at me, water dribbling from her chin. Then, obviously reflecting on life for a minute, she emitted a long, heartfelt sigh and backed away. I heard the brush of hay against her legs.

Suddenly an unreal cry erupted from the darkness. Like a stone breaking the surface of a pond, the cry shattered the stillness, spreading out in reverberating ripples and filling me with indescribable terror.

Only as it died away to a low, quavering moan could I identify it as an animal scream of terrible anguish. My heart thudding painfully in my chest, I dropped to all fours.

From the back of the stall, something was dragging itself toward me. For an instant I saw a flash of white, and then, as it came closer, I saw it was a kitten. The gray and white adventurous one. The one we called Kip.

I reached under the fence and drew it through to me. Then I saw a long trickle of blood running down my hand and, horrified, dropped the kitten back in the hay. It lay there, writhing in agony.

"Anthony!" I yelled, reaching out to stroke the little cat and wanting desperately to ease its pain. "Anthony! Ginger stepped on a kitten!"

In a moment my brother was standing over me, looking at the little creature lying in the straw.

"What'll I do?" I asked frantically. "He's hurting so bad! What can I do?"

Anthony shrugged, knowing no better than I.

I saw the mother cat, long and graceful, leap onto an apple crate to wash herself. I called her, and the kitten stumbled over to its mother, yowling piteously. She reached down to lick it, tasted blood, and drew back, puzzled. Suddenly she seemed troubled, and stopped purring.

Her other two kittens, oblivious to it all, emerged from a hole in a hay castle they had been exploring. She heard their hungry mews and started forward. When the other did not follow, but instead fell and lay gasping, she gave one last nudge and left it.

I fled the barn, running through the wet grass to my house. I didn't bother to shut the screen door, and I heard it crash against the side of the house behind me.

I found Mom sitting in the maple rocker, reading by lamplight. Breathlessly, I told her what had happened. To my dismay, she was only a little concerned. She told me she would come out to the barn later but was busy at the moment. I was silent as voices in my mind argued wildly with each other. Finally I said,

"But he's in *pain!*"

We talked longer, and Mom suggested that I kill it right away. My stomach began to hurt.

Back in the barn the kitten was screaming in agony. I could tell it was all broken inside and could never live. I kept wishing it would just die. I wanted to put it out of its misery, but how? I didn't want to hurt it any more!

Panicky, I started out of the barn again. In the doorway I met my older sister, Cyndi, coming in.

"Where's the cat?" she asked, and I showed her. She confirmed what I already knew, then spoke gently and confidently about what needed to be done. Relief washed over me in waves. I had just needed someone to help me, to tell me what to do. Together we found an old bucket and filled it with water. I lifted the little animal in and held him down. At first he was still, and then, all of a sudden, he began thrashing and squirming. The water was very cold, and I could feel the wet fur moving under my fingers.

"Cyndi! Help—I can't anymore!" And her strong, warm hand was on my arm, holding it firm.

Three minutes passed, then five, and all movement stopped. Seven minutes had passed before I finally dared to release my hand and lift it from the water. Kip's pain was gone.

We laid his body in a little field of wild flowers.

Cyndi and I walked slowly to the house. I wanted to hug her, but I was afraid to contaminate anything with my hands.

The next day when I entered Ginger's stall, a shaft of yellow sunlight coasted through the dancing, shimmering dust and landed on the bright straw. I followed its path with my eyes, and that's how I noticed the bloodstain. Trying not to dwell on it, I saddled and bridled Ginger and rode out of the barn.

On the way up the hill, I stopped at the little field where we'd left the kitten. He lay stiff and motionless, a sunny bower of goldenrod above his body. I turned Ginger away and pressed my heels into her sides.

Evening came, and with it a feeling of hollow incompleteness. In my nightgown, I sat on my bed, rocking back and forth. I needed so much to do something, write something. I stood and took my Keeping Book from its hiding place. Opening it to the first clean page, I picked up a pencil and tried to pry my thoughts free.

"Ginger stepped on the gray and white kitten the other day. It was crushed but still alive. I drowned it in a bucket. I almost couldn't do it. Cynthia held my arm down. I remember it squirming to get free! Dear God, I wanted to let it live! How I wanted to! But I couldn't!"

I was crying helplessly now, hot tears running down my cheeks and splattering the page. Were these childish words mine? Childish words to describe a childish emotion.

I wrote on. "Oh! It was the adventurous kitten. The one who loved to do everything! Why did it have to die? Dear Lord, why?" A soft, warm breeze filtered through the window screen, shaking it ever so gently. I bent my head over my writing, limp with the force of the sobs that jarred my body. I mourned for one little life that no one else would ever mourn for.

Blow softly, wind, and softly weep
My child lies forever asleep

For someone came late this day
And stole my little one away.

Sing softly, wind, sing to my son
Whose days to hear are suddenly done
Touch his eyes, once for me
The eyes that once loved to see!

Mourn softly, wind, and lowly soar
For the son of life who lives no more.
Where's flown the star that lit my sky?
Goodbye, my son, goodbye, goodbye!

ABOUT THE AUTHOR

Diane Matous lives in Penn Run, Pennsylvania, and attends the tenth grade at Penns Manor Jr./Sr. High School in Clymer, Pennsylvania. She says she loves animals and people, life, music, and laughter. One of seven children, she cares for "two dogs, cats, goats, a calf, a goose, chickens, guinea hens, and my pony."

Curse of the Sea Lord

by TRICIA OWENS

S ay one word, Prince Cathmor thought angrily, *and
I'll feed you your tongue.* He glared at the guard
expectantly, almost hopefully, but the guard said
nothing. Yet even as the prince passed by, he sensed a
silent defiance in the guard's rigid stance. The gray-
green eyes that stared from within the visored helmet
appeared to burn with accusation. And the man's hands,
curled firmly about his spear, seemed to quiver, as if
wanting to point suddenly at Cathmor and cry, *There
he is! The son of our lunatic king. See how he glares
with that wild light in his eyes? There's a bit of his father's madness in him already!*

"Fools!" The young prince scowled. They were all
traitors, he decided, as he strode up the hill to the
cliffs. When he became king, things would be different. No more whispering servants and glaring soldiers
when he came to power!

He topped the rise with an eager jump and was

buffeted by the chill breath of the sea roaring its greetings to him. The fresh wind blew his clothes tight against his body and the tangy taste of salt fell upon his lips. Screaming gulls circled overhead while, down below, sleek-bodied seals glistened on the rocks. Cathmor grinned hugely. He loved the sea. For a while he could almost forget the troubles he had left at the castle. Almost. He could sense his father's soldiers, camped several yards away, watching him with wary eyes.

Resisting the urge to berate them, he traversed the path that wound down the cliffside to the beach. The sand beneath his bare feet was warm, and the incessant roaring of the waves sought to soothe him. Still feeling hotheaded, he strode out to the water, determined to walk off the black mood that threatened to overcome him.

His temper had steadily worsened these days. He told himself it was the strain of war. In truth, though, Cathmor himself would have no great role in the anticipated war. At the first sign of trouble he would be spirited to a safehold. No, he wasn't worried about the war. His problems stemmed from another source: his father. If only the king knew how much trouble he caused for his son by acting the way he did! The king's maniacal obsession with the boat he was building— and during a time of imminent war!—made it clear why he was thought to be mad. Certainly no normal king would—

Cathmor stumbled and almost fell as his feet tangled with the body of a man lying half in and half out of the water. Gaping in astonishment, the prince bent over and turned the man onto his back. As he did so, he let out a small cry of disgust. The man's pale blue skin was slimy and covered with thin scales that came off on Cathmor's hands. Further scrutiny of the body showed that the man/thing had large eye sockets, wide nostrils, and a thin webbing of skin between fingers and toes. Cathmor tried to suppress a shudder. This thing on the ground was a Sea Child.

Cathmor had been raised on the terrifying tales of the Sea Children—how they'd steal babies from the coastal towns and drown the unfortunate fishermen who accidentally caught Sea Children in their nets. These strange denizens of the deep were said to be ungodly creatures that took pleasure in tormenting the humans they captured. Looking down on the Sea Child at his feet, Cathmor was filled with mixed emotions of fear and hatred.

For once, though, fear overrode the anger in the young prince. He took a slow step backward, then another, and was about to turn and run when a scaled hand grabbed his ankle with a sickening slap.

The Sea Child's black eyes were enormously round, seeming to bore into Cathmor's soul. "Please . . . help me!"

Cathmor shrieked and tried to jerk his ankle free. Wounded though the creature might be, its grip was unbreakable.

Panicking, Cathmor dragged them both out of the water toward land. He kicked frantically, hoping the stinging sand would force the Sea Child to let go. The steel fingers around his ankle remained firm, but the creature began making retching sounds and thrashed where it lay, its alien face distorted even more.

The realization that the Sea Child was choking filled Cathmor with triumph. He bent eagerly and threw

great handfuls of sand over the creature's face, revel-
ing in the sounds he heard. He shoveled more and
more sand until at last the Sea Child's hand fell slack
and its body no longer twitched.

The prince stepped back, elated; then the full im-
pact of what he'd just done turned him cold with disbelief. He nudged the Sea Child with his toe, praying
the creature would sit up, unharmed, and return to
the sea. But the body didn't move. It was dead. He'd
killed it.

"Nooo!" Cathmor's scream tore from his throat
and was joined by the wail of the sea. The prince col-
lapsed on the sand and lay there, eyes wide to the sky.

What seemed hours later, Cathmor stood up and
calmly dragged the Sea Child back into the water. The
prince felt strangely distant, as if he were watching
himself hide the body and was not actually doing it.
From this strange view, he saw himself run blindly from
the beach toward the castle, while behind him the sea
became turbulent and its waves tore at the cliffs. He
saw how his face was contorted with madness, how
the people he passed drew back in fear. He was out
of control, running from the invisible terror that lapped
at his heels . . .

The prince looked around himself in a daze. With
a shock, he realized that he was back in his chambers
at the castle. Vaguely, as if from a dream, he remembered only fragments of his nightmare flight. Yet the
pieces were enough to remind Cathmor of all that had
taken place earlier. He moved to the window and looked
out to sea.

The water was wild. Its once glassy surface was
now broken by rearing whitecaps that whipped across

the water with horrendous speed. The waves were as high as the base of the cliffs, tearing at their sides like some carnivorous beast, ripping the flesh away. Above the churning waters the darkening sky was thick with gray clouds. Fog crept in like slow fingers to create an eerie, distorted seascape. Gusting winds carried the sea spray up to the castle windows with the force of rain, and throughout the cold-stoned fortress the wind wailed a lament for the lost Sea Child.

Cathmor jerked away from the window and turned his back on the stormy scene. Fear and desperation gripped his heart like a fist. It was all his fault! He'd brought the wrath of the sea upon his father's kingdom and soon they would all be paying for it.

The prince's eyes darted to the door as the handle rattled. He was hoping he'd remembered to lock it when the latch clicked and the door swung open to reveal his father, the king, standing in the doorway.

As always when he saw his father, Cathmor felt torn by resentment and pity. This spindly old man with his stooping shoulders and weathered face was the very reason why Cathmor's life was miserable. Though the king's sharply etched features gave him an alert appearance, his unfocused gray eyes betrayed his madness.

Cathmor was sorry to see him.

"One of the servants said you were ill," the king began hesitantly. His gnarled fingers twisted in agitation. "Would you like me to get you something?"

Cathmor's forced smile turned into a grimace. "No. I just need to rest."

The older man nodded and looked around the sparsely decorated room as if searching for something to talk about to fill the awkward silence. Cathmor saw him notice the spray-splattered window and move to it, looking out.

"The sea is angry today," he murmured in a quiet voice. "Someone has wronged it."

Cathmor held his breath, wondering if the king knew about the Sea Child. "It's just storm-struck," he suggested. He feigned nonchalance. "It will die down, I'm certain."

The king turned from the window and shook his head at his son. "No, something is wrong. I have done something to make the sea angry with me. Even now the waves have reached the cliff tops; three soldiers have been washed into the depths."

"What!" Cathmor stared hard at his father and realized the revelation wasn't a product of his madness. *The sea is punishing us*, the prince thought. *What will stop it from carrying away the castle as well?*

His fists clenched. "Father, you have to do something. Have the soldiers build a barrier to keep the waves back. We have to protect ourselves!"

For the briefest of moments, comprehension flickered in the old man's eyes. In that brief instant the king was young again, displaying the raven-dark hair and handsome, brooding face that could have made him Cathmor's twin. Cathmor glimpsed the man his father should be and perhaps once was: strong, wise, kingly. Here was the king Cathmor would have grown to respect. But the moment was painfully brief. The hazy veil pulled back across his eyes and he was once again the incompetent king Cathmor despised. The man who stood before Cathmor was a madman. A stranger.

"I . . . I must work on my boat," the old king stammered, shuffling to the door. "Work needs to be done."

"Work does need to be done, but you're not doing it. Forget your idiotic boat and be king for once!"

A shake of the head. "I . . . work on the boat. Need to smooth the sides—"

Cathmor seized his father's arm. "Listen, old man—" he began. Then his eyes drifted to the king's robe. The rich fur was dusted with wood shavings and dirt, looking as though he'd worn it all day in his workshop. For some reason the sight of his father's disheveled robe made Cathmor laugh—a little too loudly. "It's no use." He pushed the king out the door. "Tell the true king that his son is waiting to meet him. I'm tired of talking to impostors."

The king paused and looked back, his crown tarnished and hanging awkwardly over his bony brow. He looked a thousand years old. "I'm not mad, my son," he whispered.

Cathmor opened his mouth to say something apologetic, then bit his lip and slammed the door in his father's face.

"I hate him! I hate him! I . . . hate *me*!" Cathmor released his grip on his hair and hugged himself, frightened of what he was becoming. The madness is truly in me, he despaired. I have mercilessly killed a wounded creature and tried to pretend it never happened. Now I am trying to seize the crown from my father's head. It doesn't matter that he's mad, he's still the king. My king. "I am lost," he whispered aloud.

Boom! Cathmor staggered as the floor beneath him shuddered. He could see through the window that the waves had completely washed over the cliffs and were pounding against the castle walls. There was no sign of the soldiers who had previously camped there. Probably scattered across the sea, the prince realized. He deserved to join them . . .

Sudden daring surged through his body and before he could change his mind, he dashed from the room. His race through the castle was more controlled this time but no less urgent. Time was running out. A thin coat of water had already seeped across the lower floor by the time Cathmor reached the front doors and heaved them open.

Stinging spray and winds struck his body, tearing his breath away and whipping his cape behind him like a wild bird. He shielded his eyes with one hand and slipped and slithered his way through the drenched fields.

By the time he neared what was left of the cliffs, he was bruised and soaked. He paused to look at the maelstrom around him, at the dim outline of the castle in which he had been born, and he allowed a sad smile to cross his dripping face. Shivering, muddied, the wind painful in his ears, Cathmor took a deep breath and announced himself to the raging sea.

"I'm the one you want!" he screamed, the wind shoving his words back down his throat. "I killed your Sea Child. I'm here to pay the price."

A tremendous wave crashed against the rocks a few feet in front of him. Amidst the spray of water that pelted him, Cathmor heard: "Conceited fool! Your offer is not enough!"

The prince stared out at the dark sea, searching for the owner of that intimidating voice. "I am a royal prince," he retorted, feeling absurdly humiliated. "What could be worth more than I?"

"A king."

Cathmor spun, knowing at once whom this voice belonged to. His father stood behind him, swaying in the wind, his fine fur robe now wet and stringy. His knee-high boots were coated with mud and his knotted hands were cut and bleeding from stumbling against the rocks. The king looked brittle and weak, and yet, Cathmor was astonished to see, he looked saner than he ever had before.

"What are you doing here?" Cathmor demanded. "Go back to the castle. This has nothing to do with you."

Ignoring him, the king turned and bowed slightly to the sea. "Greetings, Sea Lord. I am early but I am prepared to go."

"What is happening?" Cathmor screamed in frustration.

In answer, the king pointed to the sea. Rising from the waves like a newborn emerging from its mother burst the gigantic figure of a man. It drew itself up to tower over father and son like some unreal statue. Cathmor stepped back a pace, awed by this terrible, beautiful creature. Its glistening scaled skin was blue and its large black eyes and lipless mouth made its face strange and exotic. The creature was powerfully built with arms like tree trunks and a chest and stomach that rippled with muscles. With its fingers the Sea Lord could easily snap a man in twain.

But what caught Cathmor's attention more than the Sea Lord's physical appearance was what the creature wore. A circlet of rose coral rested across the Sea Lord's brow, and around its thickly muscled shoulders lay a dripping robe of woven seaweed. It was this robe that Cathmor's eyes were drawn to, for draped across the robe's front, like a string of decorative jewels, were the shriveled heads of Cathmor's ancestors. Generations of kings who had died at sea now bobbed like parasites on the Sea Lord's robe. The young prince felt his insides recoil as he stared at the severed heads.

"Greetings, King of Rheysdan," the Sea Lord bellowed. Its voice was deep and resonant, as if echoing from within a giant conch shell. "I accept your offer." It swung a hand across the surface of the water and immediately a wave rose, riding in the direction of the docks. "Your boat will be here shortly."

"What offer? What are you talking about?" Cathmor stomped his foot. "I demand to know!"

A thin, cold hand settled upon his shoulder and the warm breath of his father tickled his ear. "We are caught in a curse, Cathmor—you and I and all past and future kings of Rheysdan Isle. We are trapped on this island because the Sea Lord will devastate Rheysdan if we try to leave it."

"But why are we cursed? Why can't we leave?"

Out in the water the Sea Lord growled and slapped its palm down. "You are cursed because you are sons of that treacherous King Menwyn who stole my beloved!"

"It means that we are descendants of King Menwyn, the first ruler of Rheysdan Isle," Cathmor's father explained. "Hundreds of years ago King Menwyn wooed the Sea Lord's lover from her domain. She gave up her sea life to live as Queen of Rheysdan. Because of this, the jealous Sea Lord set a curse upon King Menwyn. The curse stated that for all eternity, all future kings of Rheysdan must give their lives to the sea. Not only must they sacrifice themselves, but they must do so in the prime of life, when they are the most powerful, when they are loved the most and will therefore be missed the most. It is the price the Sea Lord demands for its lover's infidelity." The hand on Cathmor's shoulder tightened. "You heard me tell the Sea Lord that I am early. This is true. My time to enter the sea would ordinarily have been weeks from now, the day after the war. That is why I spent no time preparing for the battle. I didn't need to. I was destined to win and become the most powerful king in the Five Isles, to be the most beloved. Now," he smiled gently, "I must meet my death as an unloved and unpopular king. But I am not disappointed."

"No!" Cathmor tore from his father's grip and confronted the Sea Lord. "You can't do this!" he declared, his voice sounding weak and insubstantial even to his own ears. "Who do you think we are? We aren't Menwyn. He died hundreds of years ago."

The Sea Lord shook its head, a great spray of salt water splattering the cliffs. "You carry his blood. As long as he lives, even through you, I must punish him."

The prince laughed bitterly. "You're mad. People say that my father and I are crazy but it's you who have lost your senses. Do you think you can control our lives? Do you think you hold the knife to our lifeline? Well, you don't, do you hear? We can fight you! Can't we, Father? Father?"

But the king was gone. Cathmor spun fearfully and caught sight of the old man already halfway down the cliffside.

"Stop, Father! Don't go!"

The king paused to wave briefly, then continued to

pick his way down. Cathmor cursed and scrambled down the muddy path, racing to catch up with his father.

He was too late. Already the old man was on the beach, running with amazing agility to where a boat was being carried by the waves to the shore. It was his funeral boat. Cathmor halted in disbelief as he stared at the project his father had committed almost a year to building. It was a dull, ugly vessel that rested heavily in the water, unfit for proper travel. Its hull was covered with strange dark plates hammered together like a shell of armor. The overall result was amateur-looking, nothing at all like the fantastic boat Cathmor had envisioned. He watched, stunned, as the gloomy, sailless tomb welcomed his father onto her deck.

"Father!"

The king didn't look back. He moved instead to where a torch burned in its holder by the rails. He took the torch and went below into the heart of the boat for a moment and then emerged without the torch.

"Say farewell to your father, King Cathmor!"

The prince couldn't summon a retort as he watched a wave propel the boat into deeper waters. Through his tear-blurred eyes he could see his father standing at the rails, his white hair flying behind him. He was waiting to die, waiting to breathe the dark, salty waters.

"I'm such a fool," Cathmor sobbed aloud, slumping against the rocks. "I have invited my father's death. He will die as I should, and betrayed by the one who should love him most. Forgive me, Father!"

The Sea Lord smiled at his anguished plea. "Say farewell," it repeated.

It extended a giant blue hand down to the miserable boat. As its fingers curled around the hull and lifted it out of the water, it emitted a triumphant laugh.

"King Menwyn, I have bested you again!"

The Sea Lord's strange face twisted with glee. Suddenly, though, it changed to a look of pain. Cathmor pushed to his feet as the Sea Lord howled in an inhuman voice and stared down incredulously at the small boat in its hand. The strange plates covering the hull had turned a bright red and the deck, where Cathmor's father crouched, was blackening. The Sea Lord screeched again as its fingers began to smoke and blister and the air was filled with the stench of burning flesh. With an outraged roar, the mighty Sea Lord flung the burning boat toward shore.

As the boat dashed against the cliffs and fell to the beach, Cathmor cried out. There amid the smoking wreckage, he sighted a white form, streaked with red. Heedless of the string of curses streaming from the Sea Lord, he darted toward the wreckage and kneeled beside the broken body of his father.

"I'm so sorry," the young prince sobbed, cradling his father's head in his lap. "If only I'd known about the curse earlier. I—"

His father raised a shaking finger and laid it across his son's lips. "Think no more of what could have been," he whispered. "We are together now as we should be. We are father and son at last. The time before this is forgotten."

Cathmor nodded, tears slipping from his eyes. "We are together." He glanced around him at the smoking coals in the sand. "What did you do?" he asked.

He was rewarded with a weak, bloodstained smile. "I outsmarted the Sea Lord. It never expected a boat

plated with metal and heated from the inside with burning coals." The king coughed and his fingers clutched
tightly to his crushed chest. "I had hoped the results
would be different. I had hoped we could break this
curse and escape together. Now you alone must do
it."

"I will, Father. I promise." Cathmor dashed the
tears from his eyes and bent to kiss his father on one
hollowed cheek. "I love you."

The old king smiled and for a moment his face was
free of pain. Then his breath whistled between his teeth
in a satisfied sigh . . . he was gone. A smile was on the
young prince's face as he placed the old man's arms
across his chest and stood up.

"They all die one way or another," taunted the Sea
Lord.

Cathmor pivoted on his heel and walked with determined steps to the water line. He threw his head
back confidently, and the king-light was in his eyes
when he stared up at the Sea Lord.

"I can beat you," he declared. "My father beat you
and I'll do the same. Only this time you will be the
one who dies."

The Sea Lord laughed, but without mirth. "Pitiful
mortal. I will take particular delight in your death. You
owe me two lives—your own and that of my Sea Child.
I will not forget that." Carelessly, the sea creature reached
up and plucked one of the heads from its robe. "This
is Menwyn," the creature explained. "I will replace
his rotted head with your fresh one."

Cathmor ignored the head as it was flicked past
him onto the sand. "Hear this: I will escape this island,
but you won't be alive to wish me farewell."

"Ho! Is that a challenge I hear?"

Cathmor nodded and a determined grin spread across his face. "It is a challenge. And keep this in mind, mighty Lord of the Sea: I am a madman. And madmen don't fight fair."

ABOUT THE AUTHOR

Tricia Owens lives in Bakersfield, California, where she attends North High School. She wrote this story while in the tenth grade. Her interests include volleyball, tennis, the violin, and writing. "I love delivering the speeches I've written, not to mention testing out my poetry on any sympathetic ear I can find."

Memoirs of a 13-Year-Old

by WILLIE TURNAGE

The year was 1980, a time of depressing change in our culture. The hippies were gone, the Olympics were in Moscow, and Reagan was elected. It also happened to be the most valuable year of my life. That year I learned what the world was really like, and I'll never forget the three rules I learned that I still use today.

"C'mon, Willie! Wake up! It's Saturday!"

That was my mom, the only woman on the planet who treated me like Beaver Cleaver.

"Mom, do we have to spend the whole day buying clothes?" Robbie piped in.

Robbie was my older brother who claimed three things in his life: 1) He knew everybody on the planet, 2) He knew everything cool on the planet, and 3) He knew everything. Unfortunately, he did have one advantage: at the age of ten he was bigger and stronger than my mother, and since Dad was a traveling salesman, he did practically everything he wanted to do: pushed me around, ate what he wanted to eat, never listened to Mom, pushed me around, pushed me around, and pushed me around. The only good thing about this was that I got more sympathy from Mom, and that's not much.

"Mom, can we go to the mall? Mr. Amazing will be doin' a show for TV at 3:00, and if we get there three hours early, we'll get good seats!"

"We'll see, dear."

Lesson #1: Always ask Mom. Never ask Dad.

Mr. Amazing ruled. He came on TV every day at 3:00 on Channel 17. He always did neat science tricks and taught me about spontaneous combustion in lysosomes. He tried to be funny a lot of the time, but he was rarely any good at it. This disappointed me a little, even allowing for the fact that I told worse jokes than he did. He had two kids and never yelled at them or spanked them. I thought he was the greatest living soul within the vast expanse we call the universe—until I found out The Amazing Truth about him.

"Mom! Hurry up! We're gonna be late!" Mom seemed not to care about my life at all, unless there was something in it for her.

"What's your rush? Got a hot date or something?"

Mom? What if I did? What would you do then? Well? Well? You wait and see, Mom. I'll be married by the time I'm sixteen and then you'll be sorry. I'll come and visit, and you'll say . . .

"Oh, hi, Willie! Uh, who's this?"

"My girlfriend, Mom. She's pregnant. I'm the dad."

"WHAT! Oh no!"

Then Mom will start crying and slowly build up to

a bawl until she's screaming her head off in the agony of this dreadful incident.

"Where did I go wrong, Willie? What did I do that encouraged you to do such an awful thing? Please tell me."

"You never let me see Mr. Amazing at the mall."

"WAAAAAAH!!!!!!!!!!"

"Don't worry, Mom. We'll get along."

Unfortunately, and unknown to me then, Mom was not that gullible.

"WILLIE! That's the third time I've called you. Once more and it's the board for you, mister."

Her yelling brought me out of my trance with a start.

"What do you want? I'm thinking and you won't even let me do that. Geez."

"Don't get smart with me, young man!"

Duh.

My mom loved to yell at me like that. It was like a God-given talent. I always seemed to think of a comeback, but I never said it.

Somehow, within the next thirty minutes, believe it or not, we got into Mom's car. This was the new car, a sleek Honda LX-I with automatic locks, a fuel-injected 4-cylinder engine, and power windows that I loved to move up and down, up and down, and up and down. The one disadvantage was that Mom used them against me to gain a sense of superiority.

"Mom, why'd ya do that?" My mother enjoyed this moment of power. She'd turned off the power windows, something she did often, destroying the only entertainment in reach for the next hour.

"Are we goin' to the mall?"

It was 10:23.

"Later, dear. First I want to go to the department store."

Yes, Mom, I know. She was setting a record. "Going to the department store" for thirty-four straight weeks. And every week the same routine—first the lingerie, then the skirts and blouses, and finally to top it all off, belts and other accessories. I usually ended up doing one of two things: 1) Being a good boy and following Mom around or 2) Climbing on the mannequins. I preferred the latter, probably because I could relate to these guys. Besides, I could yell at them, and they wouldn't care.

"Willie, dear, come along. My, look at the lovely clothes on the pretty statues!"

Wow. I already know all of them, Mom. They're my friends, but I guess you don't know that! Let's see, there's Fred, Bob, Joe, Pierre, and Bru—

"HEY! WHERE'S BRUCE??!!! WHAT DID YOU DO TO HIM?"

The shock of realizing Bruce was gone terrified not only me but Mom, too, along with any other ladies within a fifty-yard radius. My anger brewed within like a pot of Maxwell House. I screamed at my mother and received a very stern look. Then it hit me: Mom doesn't work here. She couldn't have done it. It must have been the salesclerk! I dashed across the store in pursuit of the woman responsible for this felony. With the grace of Laurel and Hardy, I flung myself up on the counter right in front of the sales clerk, scaring her half to death.

"You! *You* took him! I know it was you! I HATE YOU! BRUCE WAS MY BEST FRIEND AND YOU

KILLED HIM! WHAT?! HEY—WHAT'S HAPPEN-
ING? HELP!"

A hand was grabbing me firmly by the back of my
neck and dragging me out of the store. "THEY'VE
COME TO GET ME!!! STOP THE SLAUGHTER!!!
SAVE BRUCE!!!"

The police weren't taking me away (at the time I
wish they had). Mom was. That's worse. The next
hour flew by; however, it was about five months before I could sit correctly again. I still remember the
educating conversation Mom and I had.

"Why did you do that?"

WHOP! Spearheads of pain shot through me when
the first blow hit.

"Why do you persist in embarrassing me?"

WHOP! WHOP!

I thought to myself, "World peace? Maybe not."
The pain had pretty much ended after the first thirty-
two, so I didn't really care.

WHOP! WHOP!

"Don't you ever—"

WHOP!

"EVER—"

WHOP! WHOP!

"DO THAT AGAIN!!!"

By now Mom was more tired than I was. I think
she got about thirty gray hairs and many wrinkles from
this experience. She had to calm down. She was experiencing too much stress. She did have some com-
passion in her cold, frigid, tiny little heart, so I was
treated a little more delicately the rest of the day.

It was now 12:03. Lunchtime.

I particularly remember the place we went to that

day, a Chinese restaurant called Bo Bo China. As we entered, Mom ordered. "We'll have one buffet and a kid's plate."

"Mom, why do I always get a kid's plate when I eat more than you?"

"To save money, dear."

The man behind the cash register began to chuckle. Then it became a laugh, then an uproar. Why was he laughing? Was he laughing at me? Was it something I did? Something I said?

Lesson #2: At all times, weasel your way out of paying extra money. Put on a nice face during the whole thing, and don't be affected by people's reactions.

The lunch conversation was a strange one, but that's to be expected considering this was my first exposure to Chinese cuisine.

"Mom, what's this black gunk?"

"It's Moo-Goo-Gai-Pan."

"Oh." I knew that, but what *was* it?

My mind pondered her words for many minutes. Moo as in cow, Goo as in baby, Guy as in male, and Pan as in cooking utensil. Therefore, this concoction of food was a baby male cow cooked in a pan. I could just see it, frying right there on the grill, and they actually *served* it to people!

My stomach was one step ahead of me. My dignity would be shattered if I let it loose, but I couldn't stop it.

"BBBLLLLLLAAAAAAAAAHHHHHHHHH!!!!!"

Three dollars of cow buffet all over the waiter.

Lunch ended, and Mom was still pretty ticked. It was 1:00. Hopes for Mr. Amazing were dwindling. He was probably already setting up! How could I ask

Mom whether or not I could go? She'd probably yell at me some more. Wait a second, I know! Do it subtly, an allusion, calm and casual. Wait. I'd tell her that I did everything that morning just to show how much I loved her. I'd made my bed. I'd given the waiter a napkin to help him clean up. Then I'd ask. But she'd just think I was greedy and only wanted to use her as a taxi to and from the mall. Come to think of it, that *is* all I wanted.

"Mom . . ." The tension grew. Sweat trinkled down my forehead and into my eyes. How could I say it? Come on, mouth! Speak!

"Uh . . . forget it."

I chickened out. My only hope of ever seeing my hero, and I wimped out. What had become of me? Soon they'd be coming to take me away to the State Home for the Wimps. My family would reject me, my friends would hate me, and I would never see Mr. Amazing . . . ever. People would rather read *The Enquirer* than come visit me. But wait—there was a light at the end of the tunnel, an idea that grew bigger and brighter!

When in doubt—"Go!"

"MOM! I have to go to the bathroom really bad! Could you please pull over?"

"It can wait till we get home."

This woman was on to me. "No, I have to go—" we hit a bump at 60 m.p.h.—"REALLY BAD!!!!"

"Well, OK."

We pulled into the next Texaco, which happened to be only one-half mile from the mall, and I made a run for it. I ran with all my might, running and running, never looking back to see what kind of horrid expression would appear on my mother's face. And there it was, closer and closer, my goal, the place where he was, North Town Mall.

It was now 2:00.

Panting and heaving, I flung the doors open. Desperate to find a good seat (one that my mother wouldn't spot), I ran up and down the aisles, knowing she'd be there in approximately ten minutes. I found a place behind a big palm tree and waited. Nine minutes later (she must've been rushing), I saw her eyes fixed on my little, innocent, helpless, cowering body. The eyes flared with flame and anger worse than any bonfire thrown by a school with tons of spirit. I was torn in two. My mind said, "Stay here. You were bad. Face up to your punishment." My body, on the other hand, knew better. "RUN FOR YOUR LIFE! I ENJOY LIVING!"

In a state of panic I darted under the seats, groping for some sense of direction. Spinning in a whirl of confusion, I ended up at the end of an aisle, with Mom at the other end. Luckily, I didn't have to fight crowds. She did. I managed to avoid her in the Children's Outlet for several minutes, Babbages for several more minutes, and finally, Spencer's (an educational store).

It was 2:55.

The clock. Was it right? Could I be missing him, the whole reason I was risking my life? (I loved this guy.) Was I going to miss him? Heck, NO!

The race was on. People gave me weird looks when I began yelling, "DON'T START WITHOUT ME!" Apparently, Mom had sent Security to look for me, too, because there were two cops on my tail. (Mom's a Baby Boomer. She experiences too much stress. I wonder why?)

I made it back just in time. There he was, glimmering in the light—Mr. Amazing! I lived to touch the hem of his sport coat! That beige corduroy sport coat that symbolized everything he did. And YES! He was wearing his tie, the blue one with the red pinstripes. His hair was combed back, the style was definitely familiar. I stood there in awe for what seemed like hours. "MR. AMAZING!!! MR. AMAZING!!! DON'T START YET!!! WAIT FOR . . . me!"

During my state of hysteria, I had unknowingly run up on the stage, yelling.

Lesson #3: No matter who it is, never upset an apparently calm adult and expect to get out of it without a scratch.

"IT'S YOU!" I screamed in a frenzy.

"Of course it's me, kid. Now go sit down like the others."

"Don't you know me? Willie Turnage! Your biggest fan! It's ME!!!"

"Yeah, I've heard it all; get him off the stage."

"What? You . . . you . . . MOO-GOO-GAI-PAN!!!"

He did remind me of that pile of black gunk I ate at lunch; never before had I experienced such disappointment. Most kids mature at ten or eleven, but I matured right then. My life was ruined. I never looked up to anyone again. Then I had to face Mom.

Yep, that's about it. I got over it within a year or two. Since then Mom has become a happy housewife and settled down. Mr. Amazing has been canceled, and I still remember my three rules. Most stories have a moral, or are supposed to have one, so here's mine. I'll tell it to you straight so your English teachers don't have to ask you to find it:

Ask your father, not your mother.

Never give away more than you have to.
Never interfere with adults.

ABOUT THE AUTHOR

Willie Turnage lives in Garland, Texas, where he attends the ninth grade at Garland High School. Among his interests are acting (he's performed in a community theater), writing, computers, and model building.

Sisters, Friends, and Enemies

by CURTIS SITTENFELD

QUEEN OF SPADES

Watch out for jellyfish!" Sashie will yell when we bang open the screen door. We'll be carrying pails, towels around our necks, and sucking Popsicles if any are left from the night before. "And splinters," calls Aunt Terry. Jace will wave one arm in the air to let them know she heard, and then we'll go down to the dock.

Sometimes snakes are curled up by the bushes. We have to pass them because the bushes are next to the stone path that leads to the dock. They're usually long, black, pretty gross, but if you walk fast you can just pretend they're not there. When we were here last year, Sashie saw a snake her second day and she never went outside again. I'm not joking. Jace and I counted the number of times she left the house and it came to eleven. That includes going out to dinner, once to McDonald's and twice to Baby's for softshell crabs.

I think even Donald is less scared than Sashie, and

he's seven. Firstly, Sashie doesn't like being out in the country. She's not exactly what you'd call a city girl, but she likes going to movies, shops, whatever. Plus, she thinks she's too skinny and refuses to swim. About two years ago—we would never do this now—Jace and I took her bras out of her bureau and tried them on. Jace was kind of pudgy then and I had to buckle her in and then one of the straps popped because we had started laughing so hard. Just then, Sashie walked in. I almost died! Sashie was wearing this fancy purple velvet thing, it was Christmas, and her face turned about the same color as the dress. "Get out of here, you little brats!" she yelled, and of course, we did.

When we got out in the hall, Jace said, "Shut up, Miss Ironing Board." We started giggling again; I mean, it was pretty funny. But Sashie hadn't shut her door all the way and heard us. She told all the parents, and Jace and I had to go to bed at nine o'clock, even though it was Christmas Eve.

Since then, Sashie hasn't developed much, if you get what I mean. She grew her hair longer, though, which I told her looks nice. She stared at me all funny, as if to say, "Oh, yeah?" She's impossible to compliment, I swear. The thing that gets Jace and me the worst is how Sashie pretends to be perfect. She won't even admit that she's afraid of jellyfish and snakes and us seeing her dumb little body in a swimsuit. When Donald asks why she won't come to the dock, she says in a purring voice, "Oh, I like to sit in the kitchen and talk to Mom."

That's a joke and a half because everyone knows that Sashie likes my mother better than she likes her own. I've heard her say, "Aunt Paula, you understand me so perfectly." My mom says these corny things like, "You're such a great girl," or "You're my favorite niece." (Too bad for Jace, I guess.) All Sashie talks about to Aunt Terry is can she pleeeease go to California with Colleen? I swear, I feel like I know Colleen as a sister by now. I've never even laid eyes on her (except by photo—Jace and I found a picture of Sashie, Colleen, and some scrawny guy when we were looking through Sashie's wallet). But I know that Colleen is going to visit her older brother in San Diego, and Sashie wants to go, too. Colleen's brother is out of college and so cool, and all of his friends are sooooo hot. But Sashie guesses that we wouldn't know much about that, would we now? Jace and I just roll our eyes; as for me, I've had four boyfriends. Like I mentioned, Jace is a little large so she's only had one, but I found him to be pretty nice.

Anyway, Sashie wants to go to San Diego in August, and so she begs and begs. "I'll get straight A's for all of tenth grade," she wails, and Jace whispers "nerd" to me. That seems like a pretty stupid promise since Sashie already gets straight A's, but she has some idea that she's pulling the wool over Aunt Terry and Uncle Reed's eyes. She's really strange, I have to say.

Nights here we play Monopoly or watch TV. If something like "Cosby" is on, Jace and I like to see it. Unfortunately, Sashie sits in the back of the room and critiques the entire show. She's so annoying. She'll start up with, "Oh, yeah, right, like Bill Cosby would really be around the house all the time if he was a doctor," and by then the studio audience is laughing hysterically and we've missed the joke.

Once I was so mad, I said, "What *do* you like, Sashie?"

"I prefer 'Thirtysomething,' " she said, and she looked down at me from her honky nose. Jace and I made this plan to wait till "Thirtysomething" was on and then talk the whole time. When our chance finally came, we went and lay on the rug as usual, but the show was so boring and confusing that both of us fell asleep before the second commercial break. So, of course, we never got revenge.

Another thing: Sashie cheats at cards. She taught us the game of hearts, and since you need three people, we have no choice but to include her when we play. She always waits till one of us has too many of a suit and has to keep throwing them out, and then she sticks you with the queen of spades. The queen is thirteen points, unless you shoot the moon, which of course never happens when Sashie is playing. She's one of those people who has two points when everyone else has 37 or 54.

I have to be polite to all the Rowetts, though, seeing as this is their vacation place and not really mine. Last year we put a banana—a piece of fruit, for gosh sakes—in Sashie's bed and she thought it was a snake and freaked. She flicked on the lights and started bellowing until Uncle Reed came up to the kids' loft. After he scolded us and then took Donald to the bathroom, he went downstairs again, and that's when Sashie pounced. She said, "Judy Duvell, I hate you. I've hated you since you were a baby. Do you know that all the clothes you wear used to be mine, including that nightgown you have on right now? Our dad pays for you to go to private school because your dad is so lazy that he can't even stay in one job. And we let you come to this house with us, as a favor." She was really worked up by then, talking so fast, so excited to finally be telling me off that she tripped over some of the words. "You're the rudest, most obnoxious little snot I've ever met—besides maybe you, Jace—and I think it's terrible because you're just living off us." Then she let out this sigh so we'd know, even in the dark, that her Grand Speech was finished.

"Oh, be quiet, you ugly cow," Jace said, and even Donald started laughing. Sashie went to sleep on the floor of her parents' room. The next day she came down to the dock—that was one of the eleven times— while we were swimming.

"Come here, Judy," she said. I swam over. I felt pretty dumb, actually, because I remembered that the suit I had on had been hers before. It had pink ruffles across the stomach. "I'm sorry for what I said to you. I'm three years older"—of course she would stick that in—"and we're cousins, and I should know better."

"It's OK," I answered. Actually, I'd started crying after Jace and Donald fell asleep. But from the way her mouth was pinched up, I knew I'd better say it didn't matter.

"Good." Then she turned and walked her bony legs up the planks of the dock, as if she were a Southern belle.

That incident happened last summer, so I try not to think of it. Even though Sashie is as unlikable as ever, at least she doesn't say anything about my parents. They're getting a divorce now, so I'll be with the Rowetts until September, maybe longer. I might start school with Jace. We'll both be in seventh grade; I'm definitely switching schools, I just don't know where I'm going. Now it's the end of July—not much longer till Sashie might be going to San Diego. Jace and I are crossing our fingers that she stays out there for good.

Kati and Marty and Heather

When Kati signed her name, she dotted the i's with bubbly hearts. I thought they looked stupid. Kati was always trying to be a big shot. Marty and I sometimes talked about her, but then we felt bad. Once Kati made Marty cry. "Your sister is a slut," she said, pursing her lips and squinting her eyes. We were in fifth grade, but she already wore eyeliner. My mother wouldn't let me.

"No, she isn't," Marty had yelled. Her face had become all red and splotchy, like it did when Mrs. Harney called on her to read aloud in English class.

"What's a slut?" I asked, but they ignored me.

"My older brother told me so." Kati grinned wickedly. She had pointy teeth. She scared me when she was trying to be mean.

"I hate your brother," Marty said.

"Just say that to his face." Kati whirled around and left us. We were at the mall in Oakridge, and I knew that her mom was picking her up soon anyway, but Kati always tried to be dramatic.

"What's a slut?" I said to Marty.

"I don't know." She was sniffling like a little dog. I handed her some pink Kleenex from my coat pocket.

"Then why are you crying?"

"I know it's bad. I know how Kati is."

"She's just trying to be cool." I patted Marty's shoulder. I hoped she would stop bawling. People walking by looked at us like we were weird.

By seventh grade, we knew what slut meant. That's

what we called Kati, but not to her face. In gym class, she sneaked out the door in the girls' locker room and did stuff with the eighth-grade boys. For a few weeks, she was hanging around a lot with Richard Hilzen.

"Is he your boyfriend?" I asked one day. We were at her house.

"Shhh!" She looked at me sternly. "My dad's upstairs."

"Why is he home in the afternoon?"

"Because he lost his job." Kati was spreading peanut butter on a piece of Wonder bread. She accidentally stuck the knife through the slice of bread.

"Oh."

"Yeah, well . . ." She carried her plate to the table where I was sitting. "I'm sure my dad will get another job. He's really smart." She grinned at me. I couldn't tell if she believed what she was saying; if Kati felt bad, she never let you see it.

"So about Richard?"

"Nothing." She shrugged her shoulders.

"But I always see you two together."

"Like he'd go out with me." Kati gave a brittle laugh. "Like anyone would."

"Of course they would. Chad Michaels sits with us at lunch every single day."

She looked at me strangely. "He likes *you*, Heather."

Kati never gave credit to anyone. I didn't know what to say.

In November they started smoking. They liked Camel Lites, and when Jill Harrison brought in animal crackers, they all said, "Give me a camel, where are the camels? I loooove the camels!" They eyed each other like it was funny. I never smoked. My mother used to and it took her three tries before she could quit.

"Why don't you ever light up?" Marty asked me.

"Light up?"

She held an imaginary cigarette between two fingers and pretended to drag on it. "You know."

"Oh. Well, it's kind of gross."

"What?" Marty looked like someone had just told her the world is flat. "Are you serious, Heather, or are you teasing me?"

"I'm serious."

"But it's so relaxing."

The year before it would have cracked me up to hear her say that, considering that she almost coughed up a lung every time she inhaled. But now it just made me sad. "I don't know. I just don't like how it smells."

"Oh." Marty nodded her head rapidly. "I see what you mean."

The best time the three of us ever had was at Marty's sister's Sweet Sixteen party. We were the youngest ones there, and all these older guys asked us to dance. After a while, we sneaked some beer and went inside Marty's room. Everything any of us said seemed so funny. I almost peed in my pants, I was laughing so hard. We went out on the roof and yelled really loud and Kati pulled up her shirt so you could see her bra, but the music was so noisy that no one even looked at us. We were allowed to sleep in the backyard, after we helped clean up.

In the spring, my grades started to be pretty good. I don't know why; I guess the subjects were easy. My parents wanted to send me to Oakridge Country Day. And I didn't protest at all, that was the weird thing.

In June, we sat in the schoolyard and signed each

other's yearbooks. "I have a present for you," Marty told me. She looked so pleased with herself that I was afraid it would be awful and I would have to pretend that I loved it. She handed me a little square package.

"Make me look dumb," muttered Kati. I think I was the only one who heard her.

"Open it, open it!" screamed Wendy Marshall. She'd been hanging around with us a lot lately. She was always screaming.

Inside the box was a plastic picture frame with a photograph of Kati, Marty and me. Marty's mother must have taken it in the fall. We had all been on the soccer team together, before Kati quit. In the picture, we were smiling hugely, our arms slung around each other's necks, our faces flushed from the game. Across the bottom of the frame someone had written "Kati, Marty, Heather: Best friends forever." I almost started crying. When I looked up, Wendy had disappeared.

"I can't believe this," I said.

"You like it?"

"I love it." I hugged Marty, noticing uneasily how skinny she had gotten. Kati should make her eat.

"Well, my mom had the idea, but I agreed with her, you know . . ."

I nodded. "It's from me, too," Kati piped up.

"Thank you so much." I turned to hug her. She was smirking.

Kati's mother dropped me off after the class party that afternoon. Kati walked me up the driveway to the back door. "I can't believe you're really ditching us," she said and mock-frowned.

"Aw, come on. I'll be back to visit so often that you'll be sick of me."

"Sure."

"I will."

There was a silence. "So you'll be a private-school chick now."

"Ha! Never!"

"Don't turn into a snob." I knew she was trying to be serious, trying to give me helpful information.

"I won't." She raised her eyebrows, disbelieving. "I promise."

"OK." And then her face went flat, and I knew that all the times I'd thought she didn't really like me, I had been wrong. I wished she wasn't being like this. I wished she was smoking or cussing or saying she didn't care if she failed pre-algebra. We had been swimming at the class party, and our clothes, hastily pulled on over wet bathing suits, were soaked. I shivered.

"Don't forget us townies," she said. Her lips curled up. I had never seen Kati cry.

"What's a townie?" I asked dumbly.

"Jeez, Heather. You never know anything." She hugged me then, a loose, awkward hug. And then she turned away without saying goodbye or anything. I saw her shoulders shake as she retreated to her mother's car.

"Bye," I called suddenly. "I'll see you soon." But that's another weird thing: I never did see Kati or Marty after seventh grade.

ABOUT THE AUTHOR

Curtis Sittenfeld lives in Cincinnati, Ohio, and attends Groton School, a boarding school in Groton, Massachusetts. She wrote these stories while in the tenth grade. Among her interests are soccer, editing the school literary magazine, and volunteering at nursing homes.

Fish Summer

by MICHAEL LIM

I ran from the chaotic confusion which perpetually festered in our cramped house. I ran from my mother's screaming, my father's grumbling, my little brother's howling, and my baby sister's shrieking. I ran from the undone math and English homework, and I ran from the chores which haunted my conscience. And yet, looking back on that summer day's chain of events, it seems that I had been just as much running *to* somewhere as I was *from* somewhere. Each and every day I endured several hours of torturously long summer school sessions, coming home to a world of struggle and tension, only barely held in check by a certain degree of tolerance which each member of our family was forced to possess. Each day I returned home, ready to abandon my worries and enjoy the pleasures of a beautiful summer day, which I considered a fourteen-year-old's natural right, only to find that I had more homework than I could ever finish in a week, more chores than would have been necessary to drive me crazy with frustration, and more things which irritated me to the point where I had to get away before I really got into a fight with someone.

So I ran. I ran far and hard to the deserted beach which was several miles from our house. It was not a very pretty beach like some which neighbored the immediate vicinity, but it was for me a sanctuary where I could wander alone and wind down the hostility within me. It was a place to drag feet in the hot sand, a place to wade and swim within the cove's clear, sweet waters. It was a place to indulge in aimlessly walking along the water's edge, to suddenly jump backwards in order to avoid the onslaught of a particularly swift wave's crashing arrival on the sand. It was a place to completely forget about the outside world on those humid days when you felt as if you were being baked alive and browned to a crisp by the relentless sun. And it was, as I found that same summer's day, a place of many hidden and wonderful things.

"Excuse me, young man! I just asked you a question, young man! Look at me when I am speaking to you!"

A voice drifted by me like a cloud. I was unconsciously aware of the sudden, electrifying silence in the usually murmuring classroom. It was only a moment later that I floated back into the moving world and found myself face to face with a woman who reverently believed that all daydreamers were actually undercover agents for the devil himself. My summer school math teacher loomed larger than life before me, expecting an answer from me to a question I could not possibly have heard.

"Young man, I have asked you what three multiplied by twenty-seven is four times already! Your behavior is shocking! Daydreaming in class, knowing nothing of what we are presently studying, and playing dumb before the teacher for whom you should have at least a small amount of respect!" Silence. "Well, say something for yourself!" my math teacher thundered, looking to me much like a dried lungfish that hadn't seen water for centuries.

I sat still, trying desperately to recall her question.

"Three times twenty-seven?" I asked a little too timidly, even for my own liking.

My teacher gave no sign of response, save an almost imperceptible, awkward nod of her head, which made her look so uncoordinated that I had to chuckle, but I managed to avoid more of her unrestrained fury by grinning only half-heartedly.

"Three times twenty-seven, hmmmm," I mumbled, trying to look as if I was thinking very hard.

"Ninety-one?" I asked cautiously, not knowing if the answer was right.

She looked coldly at me as she pronounced the verdict. "That is incorrect. The correct answer is eighty-one. I am sending a letter home to your parents because your behavior in class is simply atrocious," she growled without skipping a beat. "You have learned nothing in spite of all my efforts, due to your abominable attitude."

I hadn't understood all of her words because she used such puff-headed language, but I had grasped enough of her message to make my resentment and impatience grow; anger and impatience at being sent to summer school, when I could be running free, enjoying myself. Personally, I couldn't have cared less if three times twenty-seven was eighty-one or five zillion and a half.

I had listened to her long speech without speaking a word, and when she was through, I simply got up and strode out of the classroom, though it was ten minutes before dismissal time. Ignoring indignant cries behind me, which could only have been hers, I walked on, head hung low, trudging along the familiar path homeward.

Upon arriving home, my thoughts shifted from school to family, and the possibility of being allowed to skip my chores and go play.

My mother emerged from the kitchen, greeting me and remarking that I was home early. I told her what had happened, and she looked upset but said nothing. I excused myself and went to my room.

That same afternoon my mother exploded, yelling at me because I hadn't closed the garbage can lid properly, and our dog tipped it over, scattering our garbage all over the neighborhood. My baby sister cut herself on a piece of glass while playing under my supervision and screamed her head off. My little brother wanted to play cowboys and Indians with me and practically deafened me by unexpectedly firing his cap gun an inch away from my ear. At three o'clock my father came home, and the first thing he told me was that I was in trouble for having used his tape deck without having first gotten permission.

All of this was too much for me to take. I burst out of the house, calling back to my mother, "I'm going for a walk!" I started to run, not waiting for a reply. I pressed forward, propelled by the frustration which had been welling up in me all day. I ran and ran in the scorching heat of the sun for about fifteen minutes before I decided to go to one of the beaches in the area, one where I knew I could be alone.

I tried to figure out the situation; I was angry because I was enrolled in summer school when I could have been playing, as most of my friends were doing. I was angry at my little brother, who had given me a headache with that infernal cap gun of his. I was angry at my mother for making me feel guilty about not having closed the trash can lid. I was angry at my baby sister for being so helpless that I had to watch her constantly. I was angry at my father for getting so upset over something so trivial as using a cassette player without first asking. It wasn't that we didn't love each other. It was not that we enjoyed making each other miserable. It was not that we didn't care about each other. It was just that . . .

All my thoughts were dispersed a moment later as I felt the hot sand of the beach upon the soles of my shoes. I took my sneakers off and slowly walked down to the water's edge. My feet tingled as the soothing water made first contact with my suffocated feet. The water was so cool and clear it seemed that it was not part of the sea, but a part of a mountain's clean, freshwater stream. I tore my shirt off and drew in and held my breath. Bravely—or rather, insanely—taking the plunge, I flung myself into the water, savoring the feeling of its gentle, pleasant movement against my skin.

After swimming for a short while, I crawled out of the water onto the sand, feeling thoroughly refreshed and a little exhausted at the same time. Sitting on the white sand, I began to notice the features of the beach with close scrutiny, realizing that it was very isolated. I had been here several times before, but it was only at this instant that I really began to acquaint myself with the place.

Facing inland, to the left and right of me on either side of the beach, were large outcroppings of jagged black rock rising several tens of feet high. Toward the ends of both sides of the beach, the rocks suddenly and violently became cliffs, sheer in angle, towering high over the sand. The cliffs jutted out into the water for several hundred feet, completely sealing the beach off from adjacent strips of seacoast.

Directly in front of me, where I had entered the beach, was a low point in the sandstone hill which encircled the part of the two-mile-long, crescent-shaped beach which was not already hemmed in by the aggressive black cliffs. The beach itself was covered with small dunes of fine, light-colored sand, which eventually turned into a steep-angled drop as they neared the water's edge. I turned around completely, so as to face out to sea, and as far as I could see, there was nothing but the same clear blue water stretching out until it blanked out of existence as it met the sky at the horizon.

I lay on my back and rested peacefully on the clean sand, now in a fairly relaxed condition, and I silently forgave my irrational math teacher, my tense parents, and my bratty younger brother and sister.

After a time, my wonder at the malignant black cliffs grew into curiosity, and I rose, put my shirt on, and walked toward the closer end of the beach with the intention of climbing the cliff, if I could find a reasonably safe path. As I drew nearer to the cliffs, however, there began to appear at the water's edge a formation of sand-white rocks which constituted a sort of miniature reef, giving shelter to a series of deep tidepools, which merged further out with larger areas also enclosed by the reef-like structure.

My urge to climb the cliff quickly diminished as my interest in a particularly large section of the described series of enclosures increased. Wading into the water, I stepped onto the elevated reef platform, which was about an inch below the water's surface. I walked up on the reef in the direction of the pool that I wanted to see. I stumbled on the slippery rocks and nearly fell a couple of times, cutting my ankles and drawing blood, although of no great consequence. My feet were constantly being poked by sharp pieces of coral, or something or other, and I tried as best as I could to keep from imagining what horrible creatures could be hiding within the numerous holes and hollows in the reef, waiting for me to make a mistake and fall into the water, helpless and ready-to-eat.

I approached my destination warily, peering into the ten-foot-deep pool cautiously. The pool was almost perfectly circular in shape, with a diameter of about twenty feet. The water was as clear as it was at the shore, and the sand at the bottom of the pool was as fine and white as flour. The surrounding coral walls were a light shade of gray. Sunlight sliced down through the water, brightly lighting up the pool.

It was the most beautiful thing I had ever seen in my fourteen years of existence. At the bottom of the pool, in the very center, was a fish, lying quietly in the otherwise empty pool. The fish was a blazing yellow with streaks of almost metallic blue running down its sides, resembling a slender torpedo in shape. It was at least several feet long, streamlined, its head and tail tapered down from its thicker body. The fish's fins and tail were the same blue as its streaks, only translucent.

As I watched the fish, I noticed that its gills were rapidly quivering, and it looked as if it were trying to calm itself. I was captivated by it, instantly mesmerized. It was almost magical; it was functional beauty, it was serene and peaceful, it was perfection, and it was, in a way . . . like me. Yes, in a very abstract way, it was like me. It had fled from the frustrations of its own world to rest in the solitude of this wonderfully fabulous refuge. Like me, it was attempting to calm its angered soul, to rest its anguished mind. And it lay there, completely still, save its fluttering gills. And I stood there, completely still, save my wildly thumping heart.

The fish seemed to raise its eyes and look at me, but showed no real sign of having done so. I had compared myself to a fish. Why? I was definitely not a fish, but I needed something, if not someone, to tell my troubles to, to confide in. I needed to see that I was not alone in this world, the only one with troubles, and I needed to know that others were needing to know all these things.

As I thought this, I watched the fish the whole time. However, I did not notice the entrance of a large, menacing, black eel. When I did notice it, it was rushing at the fish—it was rushing at me! The fish was torn to shreds in the vise of the slippery eel's needle-sharp teeth. The eel villainously slithered away into the reef, leaving a pool of blood-red water. As I stared into the pool, I began to weep. It had all happened in a split second, and I now reacted, though much too late.

I hated once again. I hated the eel, which had abruptly and mercilessly destroyed my beautiful fish, my thoughts, and a part of my soul. How could I be so worked up over such a small incident? How could I cry for the death of one common fish? How could I so passionately hate the eel, doing only what it must do in order to survive? I was sad, I was frustrated, and I was full of hate.

The answer, of course, lay right there—at the scene, at that instant. I realized that, with a slightly different emphasis, it was my question that was the answer. How could I hate over such a small incident? The point was, I couldn't afford to, because hate was too costly. I could restrain hate, endure bratty siblings, angry parents, disgruntled teachers. I could return their hate and misunderstanding with my love and understanding, and— try to live differently with this in mind.

And yet, I was extremely sad, and I sat and cried for a long time before I started for home.

I returned many times to the beach that summer after finishing chores and homework and other things. I always returned alone, though, and I always visited the same pool, and sat and waited for that blue and yellow fish.

ABOUT THE AUTHOR

Michael Lim attends the American International School in Vienna, Austria. He enjoys computers, tennis, and writing. He wrote "Fish Summer" while in the eighth grade.

Dandelion Chains

by SARAH MANVEL

There's nothing to do here; I hate it here."
"All right already! Don't you think I know it?
Stop whining."
Nessie's my best friend. She moved here two years
ago from some town in Michigan—I always forget which
one. I moved here six years ago, but besides her and
me, only about ten other kids in our grade were born
somewhere else. Me, I was born in Tacoma, Washington, a million light-years away from here.
"So are we gonna do something?"
"I don't know. Whatcha wanna do?"
"We could hang out at the Dairy Queen." Nessie's
boyfriend works at the Dairy Queen and we go there
to talk to him 'cause there's nothing else to do. I don't
like Cabe very much. He's full of himself and he spits
and smokes a lot. Menthol. And he can't keep his hands
off Nessie—I know they're sleeping together but I don't
need to be reminded of it every time I see them.

"You just wanna see Cabe." We are swinging back and forth on my sister's old white swing set in the backyard. It feels like it's gonna collapse at any moment, but me and her stepbrother Joey have tried to wreck it so many times and failed that we just gave up. All it needs, though, I think, is one big storm. Nessie has been eating nothing but apples all day. She thinks she's fat and wants to be able to look pretty in a bikini if her family goes to a beach up in Michigan.

"No, I saw him last night."

"Yeah, I bet you saw him."

"Well, what else are we gonna do? Sit here all day?" Nessie gets off the swing and throws the rest of her apple into the street. She throws like a girl.

"OK, all right. Lemme go tell Spider." I go in the house and find Spider watching game shows on TV. As usual, she's wearing all black and she still hasn't brushed her hair—it's been a couple of months. Mom tried yelling at her but you might as well yell at a pile of bricks. I tell her me and Nessie are going out. She doesn't say anything. I'd think she hasn't heard except I know her too well. Her eyes don't move from the screen and her hands are gripping the armrests like they're the lifeboat taking her away from some sinking ship. Maybe they are. She has six fingers on each hand, courtesy her daddy. He lives a couple towns over and dumps Joey off here a lot. I hate her daddy. Mom divorced him when I was little.

I go back outside, and Nessie and me decide to take the long way—Cabe's working there till six and there is absolutely nothing else for us to do. She isn't wearing shoes. As we wander up and down the streets, Nessie absent-mindedly braids her hair and tells me about her aunt in Ypsilanti who she's gonna visit next week.

Her whole family is piling into their ugly old station wagon—her mom, dad, and four little sisters—and driving the whole way there. Her dad wants a boy, which is the only reason she has so many sisters. They are the biggest brats within four counties. Mom said Nessie's mom is pregnant again, but Nessie hasn't said anything and she wouldn't, anyway. I think Mom might be right, but it's hard to tell—Nessie's mom's not exactly a Jenny Craig "after" picture, if you know what I mean. I feel sorry for her and tell her so. This aunt used to be a hippie and now lives in a big smelly house with twelve dachshunds. But it's on the water.

The streets are long and winding, and anyone who hasn't lived here for a while gets lost real quick. I spend a lot of time just wandering about. Sometimes I even sleep in people's backyards if I don't feel like going home. Mom doesn't care and even if she did, nobody'd rat on me. I took Nessie around everywhere with me when she first got here, and now she thinks she's so cool 'cause she can tell her parents she was up in the Logan tree house with me when really she was over at Cabe's.

We walk past this girl Maybelline's house where she's watching her kid splash in a wading pool. The first party Nessie ever went to here was the one that Maybelline got knocked up at. Maybelline's parents didn't care about the baby 'cause they know that sex's about the only thing to do here, but they almost threw her out when she wouldn't say who the daddy was. She couldn't remember—somebody had to tell her.

We stop and talk to her a little 'cause we don't see her too much since she dropped out. And anyway, there's no rush. The kid's wearing only his diaper and looks miserable. We've both baby-sat him. Maybelline's not exactly the best mommy. His name's Daniel, after the whiskey. Maybelline starts telling us about the last time she saw her boyfriend, and she splashes some water over the kid's head, and he swallows some of it and starts screaming and peeing, so Nessie tells her we have to go. Maybelline says, "See ya," curses, and carries him roughly inside. When she's let the door slam, I tell Nessie that that's what happens when you name your kid after your favorite kind of makeup. Nessie laughs so hard she sits down in the middle of the street. There aren't any cars driving around 'cause everyone who can drive is at work. The bottoms of her feet are black as hell.

It's getting humid so we take a shortcut across people's yards to get to the Dairy Queen. When we get there Cabe's sitting out front, smoking. He tongues Nessie anyway. I go inside to get away from them and order myself a root beer float. The floors and windows need a good hosing down. Maybe even some soap. The air conditioning feels good but sounds like it's trying to lift off. The jukebox is playing Skid Row. The girl behind the counter was in my Spanish class at school, so I gotta talk with her a little. Her boyfriend is having a party Saturday and she invites me, BYOB. I ask if I can bring a friend, Nessie maybe, but of course she'll go with Cabe, so maybe, there's this guy who was in my math class who calls sometimes. He likes me. He's OK, but not that cute. "Sure," she says, giving me a knowing look and nodding over my shoulder. I turn around and the first thing I see is Cabe sticking his hand up Nessie's shirt outside, but then I see Joey in the corner. No one else is in here. He's reading some car magazine and eating a banana split.

I sit down across from him, but he's so wrapped up in his magazine he doesn't notice me. I step on his feet to try to get his attention. "Hi, T-Rex," he says, without looking up. The first time I met him was a couple of years ago and Spider's daddy told him the story about the only time I was in a museum that wasn't 'cause of school. I was real little—I think Mom was pregnant with Spider. Anyway, we came into the dinosaur hall and I had never seen one before. They had one of those computerized ones, a *Tyrannosaurus rex*, with a tape of roars and howls and snarls playing, you know. And I stood in front of it and roared back for as long as they'd let me. They laughed at me forever 'cause I thought I was really talking to it. They used to call me T-Rex all the time, but it got kinda old so they stopped. Only Joey calls me that now. I wish he wouldn't but he's one of those people who can't change names. I was teasing Nessie the first time they met so I introduced her as Helga, and that's what Joey still calls her. She doesn't like him much. He calls Spider Spider, though. I don't think anyone calls her by her real name. That's my fault, too—I thought her hands were spiders the first time they showed her to me.

I'm getting bored, so I slurp my root beer real loud. Joey keeps right on reading. "Hang on, T-Rex, I'm almost done." I start drumming my fingers on the tabletop, but he ignores me. I give up and watch Cabe and Nessie separate and come in.

"Hey, babe," Cabe calls over to me as he lights another cigarette. I raise my hand and wiggle my fingers and smile at Nessie but not him. Nessie asks him for one and looks at me all guilty as she lights up. I stop smiling. I weigh more than she does—we checked this

morning on her mom's bathroom scale—but she's con-
vinced she's a cow. And nothing I say helps.

"Come on, there's something I gotta show ya." Joey
grabs my wrist and yanks me up toward the door. He
leaves his magazine behind. I have no idea why except
I know that he really hates Cabe, but he has a death
grip on my arm so all I can do is shrug goodbye to Nessie. She doesn't watch as the bell jingles behind us.

"Where are we going? Cabe doesn't get off work
until six." So I don't like Cabe much. And his Sexmo-
bile reeks of smoke that's sometimes too sweet. At least,
long as I'm decent to him, he drives me places and never
bitches about the gas.

"Anywhere. I don't care."

"I thought you had something to show me." No answer. "OK, then, can we at least go somewhere air-con-
ditioned?" After six years, things in a small town are
only so interesting. Joey's lucky—his town has its own
high school and daily newspaper and mini drug trade,
none of which we have. We share a high school with
the next two towns over and the paper's a weekly and
the only drug is the pot one of my old boyfriends grew
in his backyard. Sometimes I helped him water the plants.
He joined the army after graduating last
year anyway, so I'm glad I didn't stick with him.

"Well, I don't know about the air conditioning, but
we'll find something to do. Keep an open mind, T-Rex."
He always looks on the bright side. I don't know why
he comes to this little nothing town all the time.

We wander aimlessly for a long time; couple of
hours, I'd say, but neither of us has a watch on. It's gotten really humid, and he seems to have forgotten air
conditioning exists. We don't talk; I just keep asking

him what we're gonna do and he keeps on not answering me. I ask him why he came over today, and he ignores that question, too. I don't mind all the walking, but it's hot.

His arms swing funny by his side when he walks, like how you walk when you're drunk and trying to walk straight so no one will notice, except Joey doesn't drink. His hands are too big for his scrawny little arms, which reminds me that he's more like me than Spider, and it's not just 'cause we have the same number of fingers. He's not really related to either of us—he's Spider's stepbrother, and Spider is technically only my half-sister. What makes Joey's family even weirder than mine is that I'm not sure his mom is his real mother. He told me once his mom died in World War I. I think he wishes she had died. I've never met his mom in all the time I've known him, and Spider never, ever talks about what happens when she goes to visit her daddy. And on top of all that, I have no idea why Joey's over here all the time. He's technically not related to Mom or me, and he sees Spider anyway with her daddy's visitation rights. Joey would get all insulted if I asked him, and Spider doesn't talk now that she's decided she's a freak. Mom thinks it's a phase. Her daddy thinks it's a phase. Joey said to me once, "That's a real rough phase Spider's going through." I don't agree, but nobody'd listen to me.

We've drifted out of town and are walking along the interstate. Ahead of us is a huge "Certified Sod" field covered with dandelions. It looks like the yellow brick road. "Let's make dandelion chains, Joey!" I grab his fingers, pick a big patch and plop us down in the middle. It feels good to sit down. I look at my feet, and see blisters forming. Should've worn socks.

"But T-Rex, I don't know how."

"Keep an open mind, Joey; you'll figure it out." He always laughs whenever I throw his lines back in his face. I show him how to pick the tallest ones and knot them together. Since I haven't done this in years, not since recess in elementary school, it takes a few tries for us to get the hang of it. I decide to make a crown, while Joey ends up with a lei. His dandelions are tied together much looser than mine. It looks pathetic. Mine doesn't look much better. We put them on and laugh at each other as I start going off about how I'm queen of dandelions and then Joey's mouth is crushing mine in the most awkward way and I am so startled that I do not move. Almost immediately he pulls away and stares at the crushed grass where he was sitting and I clamp my mouth shut 'cause I know for a fact that he had never kissed a girl.

"My mother and Spider's father are getting divorced," he says suddenly, like how you hear those weather reports on TV—partly cloudy with a chance of rain. "When it's final, my mother and me are moving."

"Where?"

"In with my grandparents. In Portland." Portland is the nearest city with things to do, like a shopping area and some dinky little ballet companies no one ever goes to see and clubs where bands with stupid names play. It's too far away to go to very often.

"When?"

"Real soon. I gotta tell Spider since her father forgot. And you, 'cause I won't be able to come visit anymore." He looks up at me, and he looks like the little lost puppy dog I once saw on our street and took in from a thunderstorm. Mom wouldn't let me keep her. The front of his shirt is covered with mashed-up dandelions and I'm afraid they'll stain. I start to pick them off so his shirt won't get all ruined, but Joey grabs hold of my wrist—gently this time—and pulls me down into the dandelions and kisses me all over my face and arms while I lie there very still. He's been watching too many TV movies. After a while I start kissing him back so he doesn't feel bad. But then he stops, so I stop, and we just lie there without saying anything. I know he's thinking, but I'm just looking up at the clouds and wondering if I'm doing something wrong, if I should say something, if there's anything I can do. Which there isn't, not really. We don't say anything until the mosquitoes start biting.

I sit up, slap my legs, and curse all the bugs in the world. Joey sits up too, and tells me he's gonna miss me a lot, and when he gets the address please can I write or call. He doesn't look me in the eye. "Sure thing," I say too easily as I slap my arms and curse again. It's not his fault, but now I feel like a slut for letting him kiss me.

It's starting to get dark. "It's way past six."

"Nessie and Cabe ditched us long ago for sure." He groans sarcastically and I hit him. "She's my best friend and I can't help the fact that she has a scummy boyfriend."

Joey helps me stand up and then doesn't let go of my hand. I'm really being bitten and I want to scratch and slap my legs, but I let him hold my hand. He's going away, and anyway, there's calamine lotion at the house.

We walk back to my house in the dark, holding hands

all the way. No one is on the roads so none of my friends see us together. Cold leftover meatloaf and lime Jell-O are on the table. Spider is still watching TV and when I ask her when Mom's coming back, she doesn't answer. Joey tells her about her daddy and his mom, but her eyes never move from the screen. Her hands still have their death grip on the chair, but sometime during the day she filed her fingernails into twelve perfect points and painted them black. She looks like the evil queen or the wicked stepmother from some cartoon-movie. Sure. Just a phase.

I take the bowl of lime Jell-O and sit down on the floor next to Spider and start to eat it and watch the TV. The screen door slams. I get up and watch Joey start to swing on Spider's swing set. It's kinda hard to see him since the streetlight across the way is broken. He's kicking hard, like he's trying to get high enough to jump off and fly. His back is to the house, the screen door, me. I go outside and get on the other plastic swing and try to match him. We are kicking so hard I am afraid that the swing set really will fall apart this time like my old Tinkertoys when we're not even doing it on purpose. 'Cause the shaking is scaring me, I stop by dragging my heels in the dirt, leaving crooked stripes in the dust. Then Joey jumps farther than anyone ever has and really does land in the street, but he lands off-balance and falls to the ground. I don't move. He gets up slowly and turns around and faces me. There is blood running down his legs 'cause his knees are all scraped up, and his forehead and hands are bloody too. I wait for him to say something to me, 'cause I know all the gravel in his cuts has gotta hurt, but he doesn't. He just reaches up and pulls a crumpled dead dandelion out of his hair.

ABOUT THE AUTHOR

Sarah Manvel lives in Annapolis, Maryland, and is in her senior year at Severn School in Severna Park, Maryland. She reports: "During the first half of my junior year I was an exchange student in France, where I inhaled secondhand smoke and made friends from all over Europe and the U.S." Currently an editor for her school newspaper and a member of Chorale and Madrigal Choir, she has also been trying her hand at acting and is working to start a magazine. This story was born of a conversation with a friend, who described her life in a very small and rural town.

Taking Off

by KRISTEN BINCK

E lise hates takeoff. The way her body gets pushed back into the seat and her ears pop. Her stomach is queasy and she gets that awful feeling, that feeling of having no control. The other passengers on the plane don't seem to notice, acting as if flying is a perfectly normal part of their daily routine. For just a moment she is filled with anger at these calm people, wishing they would panic like she always does. Elise knows she is overreacting, knows that her plane won't crash. Her mind understands fully, yet she still worries. She can't help it; she worries a lot.

Once safely in the air, Elise tries to relax. She puts on her headphones so that the woman next to her won't try to start a conversation. She doesn't feel like talking now. Leaning back in her seat, she looks out the window and thanks God that it's not cloudy. Elise feels her muscles relax, tension draining slowly out of her.

She closes her eyes and tries to imagine what it will

be like in Washington. She doesn't care about the city itself, because all big cities are alike. Dirty, crowded, and loud, they are perfect for making her nervous. What Elise tries to imagine is what *they* will be like. The picture that Bobby, her brother, sent her looks like a page from a magazine. Tina, a tall, slightly awkward ten-year-old, is standing next to her mother, Beth. The two are very beautiful and look alike, with black hair, dark eyes, and shy smiles showing only a few blazing white teeth. Bobby is holding the baby, Christopher, on his shoulders. Though only half-brothers, the resemblance is strong because both have their father's dark coloring. Her father stands in the middle, beaming brightly, his arms around his new family. Elise thinks about how she would look standing there. Her blond hair, blue eyes, and pale skin would make it seem as though part of the picture was underdeveloped. She is her mother's daughter.

She snaps off her headset when she hears the pilot's voice on the intercom. He announces that breakfast will soon be served. Feeling how hungry she is, Elise remembers fighting with her mother over not wanting to eat a snack that morning. Her mother had been right, as usual, and although she never says "I told you so," you can always see it in her eyes.

Mom had been very nervous this morning, pestering Elise with worries and nagging her with questions. She was afraid that Elise might get lost, or that her flight would be delayed. She asked her over and over if she had remembered everything, and if she had packed her toothbrush, and if she was sure she knew where to meet her father. Elise had been angry and yelled at her mother for bothering her, but inside she was asking herself the same questions. Despite how her mother can annoy her, Elise knows how alike they really are. Bobby told her once that her father said her mother's nagging really got to him. He said she worried too much. If he stopped loving her mother because of who she was, how then will he love Elise, the image of her mother in looks and personality? Perhaps after the month is up and she returns home for school, he will be glad to see her go.

When the breakfast cart finally reaches her row, Elise chooses a hot food tray and an orange juice. The woman next to her must have eaten this morning because she only has a cup of coffee. When she sees her food, Elise is jealous of this woman for being so smart and angry with herself for not listening to her mother. The woman must have seen her staring, because she smiles a friendly smile which Elise returns politely before turning her attention to her own meal. She finishes eating quickly, partly because she is so hungry and partly because most of the food is not edible.

After the trays have been cleared away, Elise pulls out the picture of the family again. Bobby looks so happy with them, like he really belongs there. It had been such a surprise last fall when he announced that he wanted to leave. He had kept in close contact with their father ever since he had resurfaced and settled down five years ago. Bobby had even gone to visit when Christopher was born, but no one expected him to want to pick up and move during his senior year in high school. He had tried to explain that it was something he needed to do, and that it did not mean he didn't love them. Bobby was only five when their father left, but he had memories. Elise, who was three, has no memories and doesn't want any.

On her way to the bathroom, Elise almost trips over someone's bag. Her face is burning when she reaches the lavatory, and she worries that she will open the door on someone. Once inside, she worries that someone will open the door on her. She remembers how she had been angry with Bobby at first, but she knew that he would never hurt her or her mother on purpose. Still, although she never said so, Elise thinks that her mother felt that she had somehow failed. Her eyes looked sad for so long afterward. Maybe she's afraid that Elise will want to stay, too, but Elise knows that will never happen.

Back at her seat, Elise puts the picture away. She thinks about what Bobby has told her about them. Beth is nice, kind of quiet, and eager to make a good impression. She is an art buyer who is also interested in vegetarian foods and yoga. When Elise's mother heard this, she said that was the kind of person her father once called "artsy-fartsy." Their stepsister, Tina, rarely talks to Bobby because she is painfully shy. She spends a lot of time alone, reading. Christopher is adorable, but so are all two-year-olds when they aren't sick. Bobby thinks their father is really cool, and he always refers to him as Dad. Dad loves the city and eating out. He also has a new habit—spending lots of time with his kids. He picked that one up a little too late for Elise.

Elise has never known him as Dad. At home he is "my father" or "her father" or "your father." Her mother doesn't even call him Robert because they never refer to him that specifically. Dad is someone you love, and Elise doesn't love her father. Suddenly she begins to worry about what she will call him when she gets there.

Tina calls him Robert, but he wouldn't like that from his own daughter. Still, she can't bring herself to call him Dad. Maybe she can get through a month without addressing him at all.

The pilot comes on again to announce that they will begin to land soon. Elise hates landing as much as she hates taking off. Her stomach tightens and she wonders why she ever agreed to come at all. Probably because of Bobby. She missed him so much . . .

But now, as she nears National Airport, she is furious with him. She worked so hard to distance herself, to keep her father from hurting her again, and here she is on his doorstep. She won't admit, even to herself, that she wants to see them, to see what is so special about them that wasn't special about her. What made them able to tie him down when his own daughter could not.

Elise fights back a sob as the plane rushes toward the runway. She is so scared that she closes her eyes and braces herself. When she opens her eyes, the plane is on the ground, taxiing toward the airport. She had been so sure that they would crash, but they landed safely. She gathers her bags and steps off the plane, a tight knot in her stomach.

ABOUT THE AUTHOR

Kristen Binck lives in Glenwood, Maryland, and attends Glenelg High School in Glenelg, Maryland. She wrote this story while in her sophomore year. In addition to writing, Miss Binck enjoys music, reading, and sports—field hockey, lacrosse, skiing, and swimming. She plays the flute and is involved in student government and community service activities, including tutoring foreign-born students.

10-00

Story Index
By topic